SAFE HAVEN

Taking shelter from a snowstorm, Giselle Warren revisits an isolated holiday cottage, expecting it to be vacant — and walks straight into someone's home instead! Blake Conrad, the owner, has moved in after splitting with his girlfriend. In rocky circumstances of her own with her fiancé, who she suspects wants to marry her purely for her money, Giselle has been hoping for solitude in which to gather her thoughts. But this chance meeting with Blake will change both of their lives forever — after she makes him an incredible proposition . . .

EILEEN KNOWLES

SAFE HAVEN

Complete and Unabridged

LINFORD
Leicester

First published in Great Britain in 2019

First Linford Edition
published 2019

A catalogue record for this book is available
from the British Library.

ISBN 978–1–4448–4064–3

Published by
F. A. Thorpe (Publishing)
Anstey, Leicestershire

Set by Words & Graphics Ltd.
Anstey, Leicestershire
Printed and bound in Great Britain by
T. J. International Ltd., Padstow, Cornwall

This book is printed on acid-free paper

1

'Who the devil are you? What are you doing here?' They both asked the same questions almost simultaneously.

'Snap,' growled the bad tempered individual, appearing from the direction of the kitchen. It looked as if she had disturbed him in the process of washing up, as he carelessly dried his hands on the tea towel. He was a large, untidy looking individual, with a shock of dark, wavy hair turning grey at the sideburns, and the most piercing blue eyes she had ever seen. Dressed in a thick roll-neck jumper and green corduroy trousers, he seemed to fill the door opening, focusing his penetrating gaze on her. His eyes sparkled icily, his tone indisputably angry.

'Since I don't remember issuing any invitation, I think I am entitled to an explanation for this unwelcome intrusion.'

Giselle bit back an angry retort. Dropping her overnight case on the floor, her shoulders sagged with exhaustion. It had taken all her determination and stamina to battle through the snowstorm, but with the prospect of sanctuary at this isolated cottage, she'd forced herself to keep going. The sight of this overbearing, arrogant man already in residence was almost too much to bear.

'I thought . . . I assumed it would be vacant.' She sighed wearily, swaying slightly with fatigue. Now she was sheltered from the biting cold wind, her finger ends tingled and her feet were like lumps of ice. Her fashionable leather boots had been a boon, but somehow snow had managed to penetrate them and now as it melted, her nylon clad feet squelched as she tried to regain some feeling in them.

'Just who are you, and how did you get in?' The occupant of the cottage was now becoming decidedly impatient. In the tiny hallway, he seemed frighteningly large and intimidating.

She backed away, closing her eyes momentarily, as if by doing so she could summon up some reserve strength from somewhere. 'My . . . my name's, Giselle — Giselle Warren. I work — worked for Seth Hadleigh.'

An expression of partial understanding crossed the man's features, but he still looked far from amenable. 'Gave you a key did he?'

'No,' she whispered, hardly daring to face him, almost at her wits end. Unbuttoning the hood of her coat, it fell back, and she shook free her bedraggled hair, trying all the while to shake some cohesive thoughts together. Her hair hung limp and damp about her shoulders — long, tangled, jet-black curls, which she hadn't bothered to tie back like she usually did. She didn't care any more; she was past caring. 'I knew where there was one — a key that is.'

'So, you decided to break in. Then what? For heaven's sake what are you doing here in the middle of nowhere in these conditions?'

'I just needed somewhere . . . '

'Don't tell me you are running away from the Hadleighs?' he said, a touch of exasperation tinged with incredulity creeping into his voice.

Her eyes widened apprehensively. They appeared huge against her porcelain white face, but she was oblivious of the picture she painted, so pathetically helpless and childlike.

He gave her a withering look. 'I suppose you'd best take your coat off. Go on, go and get warm by the fire while I make some cocoa. You look like death warmed up.'

Giselle stood rooted to the spot. The last thing she wanted was to be alone with an unknown man in such an isolated location, but she felt so tired, both emotionally and physically. The comforting sight of the fire drew her hypnotically. She staggered over and

4

sank into an armchair, holding out her hands towards the flames, welcoming the warmth from the blazing logs as it permeated her bones. Even as she waited for the man to reappear, the heat from the fire made her so drowsy it was an effort to remain awake. Sleepily she wondered why the man was there, since it was supposed to be a holiday cottage, but she was having difficulty concentrating.

'There, drink that.' He thrust a steaming beaker into her hands.

It smelled wonderful. She drank appreciatively, cupping her hands round the beaker to stop them from shaking, and gulping a little as the hot liquid slipped down her throat and warmed her inside. It was reviving her somewhat, but she felt desperately tired, and yet wary of the man sitting opposite her.

'I lost a key last summer when I spent a few days here with the two young Hadleigh children. I thought it prudent to have a spare made. I left it under a flowerpot on the shelf in the porch. I meant to tell someone, but I forgot.'

'Did Seth sack you?'

That elicited a vehement response. 'No!' she cried. 'I quit of my own free will.'

'Since such lucrative jobs are hard to come by, I presume you had good reason.'

She flushed. 'Yes.'

The man then said with obvious reluctance, 'Well I can hardly turn out a waif like you on a night like this, so I guess I'll have to accept your story for the moment. Since you say you've been here before, you will know where the spare bedroom is, so you'd best go and get some sleep. You look all in. Have you been travelling long?'

'Most of the day. I set off soon after ten this morning — in brilliant sunshine would you believe? I didn't know snow was forecast. I nearly stopped at the motel on the motorway in view of the changing weather conditions, but decided I'd rather stay here.'

Giselle bent down to remove her boots, accepting his offer of hospitality graciously. She had no option. She didn't fancy spending the night in the car, which was her only alternative. She would probably die of hypothermia.

'Here, let me help you.' With a jerk, he pulled off her boots one by one, and stood them tidily by the fireplace.

Giselle got unsteadily to her feet. 'Thank you. I'll leave first thing in the morning.' She knew she probably couldn't even make it back to the car the state she was in. Walking through the snow had sapped her strength more than she had thought possible.

The man rose too. 'By morning we may well be snowed in. It doesn't look to be letting up unfortunately.'

With that bleak prospect, Giselle picked up her case and made her way upstairs. After paying a visit to the bathroom, and without bothering to make up the bed slumped under the duvet. She was asleep almost before her head hit the pillow, after first taking the precaution of propping a chair under the door handle. She was so exhausted not even fear of the unknown occupant could keep her awake.

The sound of someone trying to push open the door woke her. Startled and befuddled, she was all set to scream with fright when she realised where she was, and remembered what had happened.

'Just a minute,' she called, quickly pulling on her jeans before removing the offending chair.

'I thought you might like some tea.' Her host handed her a beaker.

'Thanks,' she mumbled incoherently, raking a hand through her hair in an effort to clear her befuddled brain. 'I must have overslept. I'm sorry.'

'No problem. You won't be going anywhere today.'

Giselle stared hard, and the colour drained from her face.

'Have a look outside,' her overnight

landlord growled. 'Must be a foot deep in the lane. Even a tractor would have difficulty, what with the ditches on either side.'

Giselle went to pull back the curtains, and saw the blindingly beautiful snow piled high against the hedges, filling in the ditches and the cart track back to the main road. It was a breathtaking sight, and one that normally would have captivated her. It was so peaceful and untouched, but her thoughts immediately focused on travel arrangements. She would have to borrow a shovel to dig out her car, and she berated herself for her stupidity. She should have stopped at the motel. She had been aware the snow was becoming more and more of a problem, and knew it foolhardy to continue. What a mess. She turned to apologise, only to find her benefactor had disappeared.

Hurriedly she visited the bathroom. She would love to have had a shower, but thought she'd better not since hot water might be in short supply. She gave her hair a quick brush then went downstairs to the kitchen from where she could hear breakfast being prepared. The enticing smell of the bacon cooking made her mouth water. She stood in the doorway, hovering uncertainly. The kitchen was tiny, and he was such a broad, well-made individual.

'I'm sorry, I . . . '

'Come in, sit down.' He barked it out like an order, and since she was decidedly hungry, she took a seat at one of the place settings feeling like an immature schoolgirl. She wasn't going to pass up the offer of food when she didn't know when she would get another meal. Giselle sat nervously watching as he deftly slid the eggs on to plates, and added bacon from the grill pan. He seemed so competent, but with several days' stubble, and his hair rakishly unkempt, the man looked somewhat menacing, so she daren't offer to help.

'When we've eaten you can go into

more details about your plight. It rather looks as if we have plenty of time. The forecast is for more snow to come according to the radio, although they aren't always right in this neck of the woods. From the look of the clouds I wouldn't expect a whole lot more.'

'I don't even know your name,' she said quietly. 'Not Sir Galahad I presume?'

'Hardly.' His mouth twisted in a grimace of a smile. 'Blake Conrad's the name.' He put a plate of eggs and bacon in front of her. 'There, eat that while it's hot.'

'It looks great. Thanks. I'm really sorry I disturbed you last night. I realise now that I shouldn't have come without checking first, but it was a spur of the moment thing and there's no phone here is there?'

'I guess we all make mistakes,' he retorted, casually reaching over to rescue the toast before it burned to a cinder. 'Sometimes they prove to be more costly than others though.'

Giselle ate ravenously. She'd had little to eat the previous day, which was probably why she had felt so exhausted. She had spent over two hours stationary on the motorway due to a traffic accident, and then when she reached the service area it was so busy she had settled for coffee and sausage roll. The journey had seemed never ending. Fortunately her table companion also had a healthy appetite so she didn't feel embarrassed, and since neither of them seemed in the mood for idle chitchat, only the hum of the refrigerator and a clock ticking disturbed the silence. After helping herself to several slices of toast and marmalade, Giselle felt more human and decided it was time to be leaving no matter what he said to the contrary.

'I'll go and pack my bag then I'll be on my way,' she said scrambling to her feet, wondering what she ought to do about paying for his hospitality. She wouldn't like to offend him.

'You'll not get far today, not in this

stuff. It's snowing again already, so you may as well accept the fact that you're here for a while. They won't bother to clear the road down to the village, and from the look of the lane outside it will be impassable. The snow plough only concentrates on the main roads.'

'Surely it's not that bad! There must be somewhere I can stay — the pub maybe?' She glanced out of the window seeking inspiration. 'I knew I shouldn't have come . . . '

Blake Conrad sat back and looked across at her, making her feel self-conscious as she grasped the back of the chair. She was uncertain of her next move. Well aware of her foolishness, she wished to escape any further censure, but realised he was probably being practical.

'For goodness sake stop saying you're sorry. Sit down and have another cup of tea. You look as if a puff of wind would blow you away, so it's no place for you out there. Tell me why you came here of all places? Why do you wish to escape?

A young woman like you should have everything going for you — the world at your feet.'

Giselle returned to her seat. He made everything sound like an order to be obeyed without question. Was he a schoolmaster? she wondered. When she didn't reply, he asked how she got the name Giselle.

'My grandmother was French and mother liked the ballet,' she murmured.

'In truth it suits you. You're like a young gazelle, with your wide, innocent eyes.'

Giselle scowled. 'I am sick and tired of everyone thinking of me as a child. I'm a grown woman believe it or not, quite capable of earning my own living.'

'Oh, I believe you,' he chuckled. 'Do you know, I've never met anyone with violet coloured eyes before. You must know you are extremely attractive, but you also have a certain air of intrigue about you. I find you difficult to fathom. So, tell me, what's the trouble?'

She chewed her bottom lip. She did

owe him an explanation. He'd been extremely kind in the circumstances, and she may need his assistance to get her car going. Better not to antagonise him. 'I've been Seth Hadleigh's secretary, or I should say personal assistant, for just over two years — a job I enjoyed, actually, although it wasn't very taxing. I was Jill of all trades, you know the sort of thing, even looking after the children occasionally. Then about seven months ago his eldest son Leo turned up. He'd been backpacking round the world, or so he said. To cut a long story short, he took a fancy to me and I rather liked the look of him. We started going out together — with Seth Hadleigh's approval I might add. We got engaged two months later, on Leo's twenty-third birthday.'

She paused, but Blake remained impassive. 'Very soon there were problems, because I wanted to postpone the wedding plans for a while. Everything seemed so . . . so rushed, but Leo was keen — eager for us to marry as soon as possible, and kept urging me to name a date.' She shrugged her shoulders, not sure how to explain further. Fortunately, he didn't press her.

'Why come here of all places? Why not go home?' Blake asked, pouring himself another cup of tea.

She was glad to change the subject. 'My father is out of the country — he's away a lot, so there was not much use going there. In any case, I feel I should stand on my own two feet. I can't keep running back home when things become difficult.' She collected the dirty plates and took them to the sink. 'I don't like staying at hotels on my own, and I remembered this place, which I felt would give me the solitude I was needing. Just until I could sort out my thoughts and feelings, you know.'

'No other family you could turn to?'

Running water into the sink, she replied, 'My mother left home three years ago, and lives with her lover in the south of France. I have a brother, Jason.

16

He's in the army so I don't see him very often either.'

He approached her with his cup and saucer. 'How old are you, Giselle? Seventeen? Eighteen?'

'I'm nearly twenty-one,' she snapped. 'I'll show you my birth certificate if you don't believe me.'

He smiled and picked up the tea towel. 'I was going to say you look young enough to be my daughter if I had one, but I'm not that old! Anyway, for what it's worth, I'm not an ogre, even if that was the impression I gave you. You took me by surprise that's all.'

'I know . . . I realise . . . I shouldn't have come . . . '

He placed a hand on her shoulder. 'You should thank your lucky stars it was me here, and not some homicidal maniac.'

2

Giselle wiped clear a section of the bedroom window sufficiently to see out. She was trying to decide what to do. Blake assumed she would have to stay in view of the depth of snow, but she felt uncomfortable being there alone with him. It wouldn't have been so bad if he had a wife or a near neighbour even, but there was no one in earshot. Finally, she made up her mind that somehow or other she had to get to the village. At least she should get to a phone so she could ring Jason, not that he could do anything to help. She wished she had listened to the weather forecast then she wouldn't be in this predicament. She could have stopped earlier or even gone home.

She re-packed her case, and when she heard Blake go into the backyard, she made a dash for the front door.

That was her undoing, too much haste. Her feet became entangled in the square of carpet at the top of the stairs, and down she went head over heels. Her case crashed after her, springing open and scattering its contents. Giselle lay winded in an ungainly heap, and fearful of the consequences. She heard the back door slam and the next minute Blake stood over her.

'What the devil? What the dickens is going on now? Don't tell me! You were going to hike back to the village despite what I told you, and now you've come a cropper. Holy mackerel what's the matter with you, child? Have you no sense? Come on give me your hand.'

Giselle shrank back close to tears.

'I don't bite,' he snarled. With a smothered oath, he put down the basket of logs and scooped her up in his arms as if she weighed eight pounds not eight stone, and carried her over to the settee. 'What's the damage?'

Without warning her eyes filled with tears and to her dismay, she found she couldn't stop herself from crying. It was all too much. Why did everything have to be so complicated?

'All right. All right. I'm sorry. Here, have my hanky.' Blake went to gather up the clothes, shoving them back in the case before returning to the settee. 'I'm sorry if I was abrupt. How badly are you hurt?'

Giselle took a deep breath. 'I think I've ricked my ankle.' She tried to stifle a sob of despair and it ended up as a hiccough. 'I caught it on the banister.'

'Let's see.' With infinite care, he investigated her foot, gently manipulating it. His touch was gentle but thorough, and she winced visibly when he found a tender spot. 'I'm afraid you're right. I don't think there are any bones broken thankfully, but you'll need to keep your weight off it for a day or two.' Blake's voice softened. He half smiled and shook his head as if reprimanding a child. 'Will you make a bargain with me? No more heroics. You are welcome to stay until the weather relents, and I promise I'll not try to seduce you, on my word of honour. I've got problems enough without having enraged boyfriends or fathers with shotguns coming after me.'

Giselle, trapped by her own incompetence and stupidity, accepted gratefully. 'I'll gladly do anything I can to help while I'm here,' she muttered. It wasn't like her to feel so inept. 'I'm not usually so clumsy. I don't know what's come over me.'

'Obviously fate is playing a hand here, so we may as well make the best of it. Now, no more apologising, ok?'

'Ok,' she replied with a wan smile.

He stroked his chin thoughtfully. 'I'm not sure what we can do about this ankle though. It could do with strapping up, but I don't believe there's a first aid box around here.' He went to the sideboard and rummaged around in the drawers.

'I have one in my car,' she volunteered hesitantly.

'All right, let me have your keys. I'll

go and fetch it.'

Giselle fumbled in her pocket and said sheepishly, 'I sort of parked it in a field gateway just past the entrance to the lane. I found I'd missed the turning and I couldn't turn round.'

Blake pulled on a sheepskin jacket and boots. 'Promise me you'll stay right there until I get back? We don't want any more accidents. Ok?'

Once he'd set off, Giselle flopped against the cushions feeling as if a weight had been taken off her shoulders. She had sought seclusion to re-evaluate her life, and now here she was, stuck for the next couple of days. Perfect. When he relaxed his aggressive stance Blake Conrad was quite agreeable company, and she thought, without his stubbly beard he would probably be quite attractive. One would hardly call him handsome. His nose was too long and his eyebrows too heavy, but he had a certain appeal if you liked the strong, domineering type. She was going to have to trust him now, and strangely enough, she did. Even though her faith in the male of the species had been badly crushed of late, somehow she knew Blake wouldn't let her down.

She hoped her ankle wouldn't incapacitate her for more than a day or two though, as she didn't want to abuse his kindness. In a way, he reminded her of Jason. Perhaps it was the masterful way he ordered her about she mused, or maybe his physical size. Not as tall as her brother, but broad shouldered like him — a strong, muscular man, and slightly intimidating. She felt certain she wouldn't be able to twist him round her little finger like she did her brother though.

It was a good twenty minutes later when she heard him knocking the snow from his boots and he entered the back door. He came into the sitting room rubbing his hands together, and squatted by the fire to warm them.

'You left the lights on. The battery's flat.'

'Oh no!' she groaned. 'I was so tired

last night I didn't know what I was doing.'

'Not to worry, we can jump start it with mine once the snow melts sufficiently to get it down the lane. Shouldn't be a problem.'

Giselle took the first aid kit and found an elastic bandage. Her foot felt much easier once that was applied. While she was attending to it, Blake made some coffee and settled in the chair by the fireside.

'What other accomplishments do you have,' he asked with a wry grin, 'beside breaking and entering I mean?'

Ignoring his sarcasm, she replied somewhat haughtily. 'I'm a competent secretary, and I have basic bookkeeping and computer skills. I can cook, sew, and do gardening, decorating, and even ride a motorbike. I can play the piano and swim like a fish. What about you? What do you do?'

He didn't take offence at such a direct question like she might have expected, but merely chuckled and relieved her of the beaker, before settling back in his chair. 'That's quite a resume. Me? Well, until recently I managed a hotel in the Lake District, but now I am what actors would call resting.'

'So what happened? Why did you come here now?' she asked. 'I never expected anyone would come to such an isolated cottage so near Christmas.'

'Divorce is what happened. My ex has a smart lawyer whose middle name is Scrooge, so by the time they've finished with all the legal niceties, I'll be left with nothing but this cottage.'

She raised her eyebrows. 'I didn't realise you owned it. I thought it belonged to the Hadleighs.'

He shook his head. 'No. Safe Haven is my home — where I was brought up. The place I return to when life gets difficult. Its sheer simplicity has a calming influence on me. Away from the world's hurly burly it's here I can reflect on life. I'm back this time though to decide on where I go career-wise. Also, to regain some self-respect. These last few weeks have completely demoralised me, so I'm not best prepared for the inevitable forth-coming job interviews.'

'I know what you mean. This place, despite, or because of, its simplicity is sort of therapeutic. I found it wonder-fully relaxing when I came here before. I didn't know it was called Safe Haven. I like that. It's nice. It suits it.'

'The board disintegrated some time ago, and I haven't got round to replacing it. I fancied making it out of driftwood.'

Giselle chewed her lip again trying to understand all he'd been through. Splitting up, as she knew from when her parents separated, could be very traumatic, but to lose everything must be terrible.

'No children, then?' she asked cau-tiously, feeling nosey and not sure if he would be prepared to disclose such personal details.

He shook his head.

She felt sympathetic, so decided to interrogate further. 'What happened to your job? Why . . . '

'My precious in-laws owned the hotel, although they hardly set foot in it from one year end to the next. Marie — my nearly ex-wife — and I managed it on their behalf. It seemed like a good idea at the time. A job, a roof over our heads, plenty of work, and money we could put by towards our own home when we started a family. I was living in a dream world. I can see that now. Marie never managed to cut herself free from her mother's apron strings. She was always a shade immature, but in a way it was what I found attractive about her. Looking back I can see we were not well suited. Hindsight is a wonderful thing. Anyway, enough about that, soon I shall be a free man again, with no assets apart from my own wee cottage. Thank goodness this is something Marie and her folks can't get their grasping hands on.'

Giselle wanted to ask why they split

up, but couldn't find the right words. 'I'm sorry,' she said finally. 'Life doesn't seem fair at times does it?'

'Huh, you can say that again,' he growled prodding the fire viciously.

'Have you any ideas about what you want to do now?' she asked after a while.

'Get a job somewhere.' He shrugged his shoulders. 'When I'm good and ready.'

'In the hotel trade?'

'I suppose so. It's what I know best, but I really haven't given it a great deal of thought as yet. What about you?' he asked, clearly not wanting to pursue that topic. 'Will you be looking for other employment?'

She smiled. 'I guess so, although I'm in no hurry either.'

He quirked an eyebrow enquiringly.

She decided he deserved to know a little more about his unwelcome visitor. 'I like Leo, of course I do. I wouldn't have got engaged to him otherwise, but . . . oh, I don't know. I needed time to think, and this seemed just the place. I came here with the Hadleigh's two youngest children last summer while their parents were abroad on business. We had a great time, but like I said, I thought it was a holiday cottage, and didn't expect it to be inhabited at this time of the year.'

He chuckled. 'I was a bit surprised when Seth rang me, quite out of the blue, to ask if they could rent the cottage last summer. Now I understand. I didn't think this was his idea of holiday accommodation.'

'I didn't know you knew them.'

'Oh, we're not exactly bosom pals. I've not seen Seth for donkeys' years. The Hadleigh family used to holiday in the village many years ago, before they acquired their wealth, and my dad used to take them out on fishing trips. There were three boys. Seth was the eldest and I was about the same age as his youngest brother. I used to tag along with them sometimes when I had nothing better to do. I believe my parents kept in touch with them with the usual Christmas card message and so on, but since they died, I'd lost touch.'

He rubbed his hands together and got to his feet. 'Well now, I'm afraid there's not much in the way of amusement around here. The radio is more or less workable, and there are plenty of books, but obviously no television. It's like stepping back in time isn't it? Not quite your usual cup of tea I dare say.'

'Suits me fine,' Giselle replied, grinning happily. 'Even my mobile phone doesn't work here. It's as you say, like being in a time warp and the outside world might not even exist. It's exactly what I need right now.'

3

The steady drip, drip, drip of melting snow greeted her the next morning. When Giselle looked out of the window, she saw Blake making a path round to the lean-to shed where he must have garaged his car. She watched him for a while impressed by the methodical way he worked, making it appear so effortless. The thaw had come sooner than expected. Maybe he would want her to leave later that day — if they could get her car started. Then what was she going to do? Go home? That didn't appeal. She needed sustenance then maybe the thought processes will kick in and suggest something. Her father always said '*Go with the flow and gut instinct, something usually turns up to point you in the right direction.*' Well now was a good time for it to turn up.

Quickly rummaging out a tracksuit, she limped downstairs to prepare breakfast. She wondered how long Blake had been up and why she hadn't heard him. For such a large man he was surprisingly light on his feet. Strange, she thought, how she had revised her first impression of him, but of course, she hadn't been thinking rationally on their first acquaintance.

'Good morning,' Blake said, arriving at the back door. 'I thought I caught the appetising aroma of bacon cooking. Did you sleep well? I hope your foot didn't keep you awake?'

'Fine, thanks. It must be the sea air. I slept like a top. I don't usually lie in so late. The swelling has gone down and my foot feels much easier this morning. I'll be able to drive, I think.'

'Don't go putting too much weight on it too soon. There's no panic about you leaving as far as I'm concerned.'

She smiled her thanks. 'Breakfast is about ready. It rather looks like a quick thaw is on the way, doesn't it?'

Blake padded into the kitchen in his stocking feet to wash his hands at the sink. 'I'll have a go at getting your car started after breakfast and bring it back to the house. The lane doesn't look too bad, but I'm not sure it's suitable for your wheels. I'm surprised you managed to get this far in yon sports car. They are not the easiest thing to handle in these conditions.'

'Yes, I know what you mean, but it wasn't too bad until the last mile or so. I could kick myself for leaving the lights on, though.'

Blake didn't make any response, for which she was grateful, and she popped the bread in the toaster relieved by his acceptance of her remorse. She felt he was being exceedingly charitable under the circumstances. Jason would have jeered at her stupidity and made the usual acid comments about women drivers, in a brotherly way of course.

Immediately after breakfast, Blake backed his car — an old estate car — out of the lean-to and drove down the track, while Giselle watched anxiously from the sitting room window. She knew her car could be a little temperamental at times and hoped this wasn't going to be one of them. She was used to its idiosyncrasies and had learned how to coax it to life, but she hadn't felt like explaining it to Blake. He would have thought her simple-minded probably. Occasionally she wished she'd accepted her father's offer of a new car, especially when her own let her down, but underneath knew she was right. She was determined to be seen as a person in her own right and not just her father's daughter, living off his wealth. Besides, she loved her MX5, even if it was a few years old. She'd rather have it than a brand spanking new sedate little saloon that her father would have had her drive. Unfortunately, it wasn't too cooperative in snowy conditions as Blake mentioned.

Blake was gone for quite some time. She wished she had gone with him. She had offered, but he had dismissed her assistance in typical chauvinistic manner. Nearly half an hour went by before she saw his car returning — no MX5.

'We'll have to tow it,' he said with a frown. 'You'll have to give me a hand I'm afraid. Do you think you can manage to get your boots on?'

'Yes, I think so.'

She was about to ask what the trouble was, but diplomatically refrained because she wouldn't have been any the wiser if he told her. Men always made everything sound so technical and complicated. They never explain in words of one syllable, and although she was quite knowledgeable about how the engine worked, she didn't know the correct names for the components. She had spent many hours passing spanners to Jason when he tinkered with his beloved motor-bikes and learned a lot in the process.

It was a bit of a struggle, but she managed in the end to push her bandaged foot into the boot and hobbled outside. Blake was waiting to ferry her down the track. She watched anxiously from the passenger seat, thinking about the ditches at the side hidden by the snow. If they dropped a wheel into one they would be well and truly stuck. Installed behind the wheel of her own car Blake gave her meticulous instructions on how to cope with being towed. 'Try to follow in my wheel tracks and keep the tow-rope taut, ok? First, I'm going to push it out into the road so that we can turn it round. You steer on my command.'

She nodded grimly and refrained from mentioning she had been driving since she was seventeen without an accident — a better record than her brother's, in fact. Blake's attitude was typical of the men she encountered, but in this instance, she didn't want to cause friction, so bit her tongue. Once they had reversed out on to the road and were heading in the right direction he hitched up the tow-rope. Then, with a thumbs-up sign, they set off. It was quite a tricky operation as both cars slithered in the slush, but Giselle was determined to succeed, to prove she wasn't hopeless at everything. She had one anxious moment when the tow-rope went slack and she nearly ran over it. She was cursing silently when the car jerked forward again and miraculously she managed to steer a true course. They finally pulled up outside the cottage without mishap.

'Well done, I couldn't have done better myself. Off you go inside and get warmed up while I'll sort out the cars.'

Giselle went into the cottage delighted by his praise. Somehow, his approval meant a lot even though she could, and should have contacted the nearest garage for assistance. Heaven knows when they would have got to her though.

During lunch, they got talking about property prices, and Blake mentioned that Marie's family was putting the hotel on the market.

'Apparently they have in mind some

new venture in Spain like so many British people. I'm not sure how viable that will turn out to be, because they say they have no intention of learning Spanish. They aren't particularly good managers and are what I can only call work-shy. They are probably looking for an easy life while everyone else does the work. I'm not sure how that will go down in Spain.'

'And Marie? Is she going with them?'

'I expect she will, although the last I heard she wasn't overly keen. The sun makes her uncomfortable. Being a redhead, she doesn't tan easily, but she'll go along with what her parents decree I imagine. She's not cut out for life on her own.'

This information gave Giselle an idea. She didn't say anything to Blake, but let it vegetate for most of the afternoon. She pretended to read, but never turned a page, her mind was otherwise employed. She knew how she could solve both her own and Blake's current career problems, but was unsure how Blake would react. She knew she would have to be extremely tactful, but the more she thought about it the more she felt it would be ideal. She rather thought when Leo heard he would be appalled, but that wasn't going to deter her. She certainly didn't want to be pressurised by him, and definitely wanted to decide her future for herself. But maybe, just maybe the gods were smiling on her and the answer to her problem was staring her in the face.

4

During the evening Giselle sat quietly gazing into the fire hugging a mug of coffee, still undecided on how to broach her proposition. She knew he would think she had taken leave of her senses, and she had to admit if the positions were reversed, she would take some convincing she was serious. However, the more she thought about it the more she liked the idea. It seemed so simple and uncomplicated that he would have a hard job finding a reason not to accept. Finally she thought she had come up with the right words to tempt him.

Blake brought in more logs and commented on her studious mood.

'I've a proposal to put to you, Blake. Please, will you hear me out? You might think I'm a lunatic or taken leave of my senses, but I assure you I'm not and I haven't. I'm perfectly serious.'

He looked puzzled, but nodded for her to continue and settled in the armchair.

Giselle took a deep breath. 'I should first of all explain my father is Bunny Warren. I don't know if you've heard of him?'

Blake's eyebrows shot up. 'Not *the* Bunny Warren? The hotel magnate? Good God! You're kidding surely?'

Giselle nodded. 'Afraid not.'

Blake whistled through his teeth and looked stunned. 'Then why . . . ?'

'You will probably think I'm stupid like all the rest,' she said with a sigh. 'Just because I'm an heiress doesn't mean I don't want to do something with my life. Ever since I left school, I've felt I needed to prove something to myself. You can imagine what it was like with a father like mine. So, I sort of rebelled and left school when I was sixteen. Obviously, I had no need of a job so I took myself off to America to stay with some cousins. Then I hopped

41

over to visit a friend in New Zealand. I was sort of back packing the easy way, and just enjoying myself. At first, it was great and I had a whale of a time, but very soon, it became tiresome and boring. The problem was I just couldn't decide what I did want to do. Back home again I took a course on secretarial work and home economics, and eventually got the job with Seth Hadleigh.

'I was feeling decidedly chuffed with myself thinking I had achieved it on my own merits, believing he didn't know who I was. I found out much later I was wrong. Apparently, he knew who I was all the time, and I think now he is conspiring with my father. I suspect, though I have no proof, that Seth contacted his son Leo and told him to return home pronto and to make a play for me. I, like a dim-witted fool, fell for it. Leo can be unbelievably charming, but I suspect my inheritance is really what he's interested in.' She grimaced and shrugged her shoulders.

'Anyway, to cut a long story short — I'm getting good at that aren't I? — soon I shall be twenty-one, which is when I inherit a very large sum of money from my maternal grandma. I've been wondering what on earth I should do with it. I know it may seem strange to you, but to me it's a dilemma. I don't want to go to the financial experts my father would no doubt urge me to use. I don't want to invest it and live off the interest, which I know I could do. I want to do something worthwhile. I just couldn't decide what.' She paused with a sigh.

'At first I was thinking along more charitable lines, but now ... I've concluded I'd like to buy a hotel — your hotel. And if I do, I'll need your help. I've been around hotels all my life, but strangely enough, I don't think I could manage one alone — at least not straight away. What do you say? It would be one in the eye for your ex-wife and her parents wouldn't it? I'd also like to prove my father isn't the only one to make a success in the hotel industry. I'd like him to be proud of my initiative. This looks like a golden opportunity, and like you said earlier, it's like fate showing us the way.'

Blake sat for quite some time gazing into the fire. Finally, looking suitably stunned, he said, 'I . . . I don't know what to say, Giselle. You've taken me completely by surprise. I had no idea I was entertaining such illustrious company. I can't get over the fact you're an heiress, and yet you wanted to hide away here in my primitive abode.'

'But you'll do it won't you?' Giselle said grinning with enthusiasm. 'Dad will be tickled pink with the idea, I'm sure, once he gets over the shock.'

Blake chuckled. 'You really are incredible. How do you know it would be a good investment? You know next to nothing about me. I might be as big a rogue as your boyfriend, and only after your money . . . '

Giselle interrupted him. 'No way. You thought I was a naïve child, remember?

Moreover, as for it being a good investment — we'll just have to make damned sure we get the best deal possible. I do know a little about buying and selling property. It's something I've always been interested in, something I learned from my father. Now, I'd like to know all about the hotel. What's it called? I can't wait to see it. What's it likely to cost to buy, and does it need renovating? Is it open all year round? How many rooms?'

'Hold your horses. Let me get my head round this. You are seriously considering buying a hotel without having seen it, or even knowing the first thing about it? You've only known about it for less than twenty four hours.'

'I couldn't be more serious. I have a gut feeling this was fate. You know the hotel. You would know what the prospects are for it to be a profitable investment. It's just the sort of project I need to get my teeth into right now. It's heaven sent.'

'What about your fiancé? What's he

going to say when he hears about such a hare-brained scheme?'

Giselle laughed. 'It's not a hare-brained scheme and as far as I'm concerned Leo is history . . . I'll deal with him in my own good time. Just concentrate on how we go about buying the hotel at the best price. We'll have to set wheels in motion straight away, as I am due to fly out to the Bahamas for Christmas. That's something I can't get out of, I'm afraid, much as I'd like to.'

He took a lot of convincing, but eventually, recognising her obstinacy and determination, he agreed to discuss it as a possible solution to both their problems. After that, they spent hours discussing the next step. Blake drew her sketches of the floor plans of Beech-croft, and told her all about the hotel — all its faults as well as its good points. He didn't want her getting carried away with some rose-tinted picture she'd created in her mind, only to be terribly disappointed when she finally saw it. The few photos he had to show her didn't emphasise the shabby paintwork or rotten woodwork. He did his best to tell her what would need doing to bring it up to the standard he imagined she would expect, being Bunny Warren's daughter. Giselle wasn't easily put off. She made a list of the possible areas that would need to be attended to before the season, especially if they were to re-open for Easter, which was their intention.

Blake did his best to dissuade her, by suggesting she talk it over with her father or Seth Hadleigh, but she would have none of it. The more he tried to talk her out of it the more determined she seemed to be to go ahead, even saying she would go it alone if she had to. In the end he agreed to be her partner in the venture and hoped he could keep her feet on the ground.

* * *

Fortunately, the thaw continued and Giselle left the cottage two days later to make a flying visit to the Lake District before jetting off to spend Christmas with her father. Blake offered to go with her to show her round the hotel, but she said she preferred to see it for herself and she would let him know what her first impressions were. He reiterated if she was at all doubtful about the proposal when she'd had time to have second thoughts then he would understand. It wasn't something they could pursue unless they were absolutely sure it could succeed and was what they both wanted. He hoped they weren't being carried away with her optimism.

When she first caught sight of Beechcroft, Giselle was disappointed, and immediately began to doubt her impulsive decision. It was definitely nothing like her father's hotels, and in the gloomy December weather it looked none too appealing. Pulling into the car park, she had a heart stopping moment when she felt she had made a huge mistake and dreaded reneging on the deal. Taking a deep breath she pulled herself together. Obviously, she wasn't seeing it at its best. What was it her father used to say — don't look at what is there now, but look beyond at what you would like to see. See the potential.

Ok. Well for one thing, it didn't look nearly as big as she had thought, but maybe there was room for extending. It was definitely in need of a coat of paint, but that was not a problem. She liked the location. Stepping out of the car she wandered over to peer in the windows and saw a reasonably large entrance hall and reception area that looked not too bad. A pleasant curved staircase led off, and Blake had told her there was a lift. Maybe freshly decorated and new carpeting etc it could be made more attractive. Yes, there were possibilities thank goodness. Perhaps it wasn't such a bad risk after all. The Lake District was highly desirable she knew, because her father had mentioned it often enough although to date he hadn't acquired property there yet.

Wandering round to the rear of the hotel she found a large grassed area with adequate space for the conservatory extension Blake had suggested, and perhaps a hot tub or swimming pool perhaps? They had still to agree which was appropriate and cost effective. A sudden shower of rain sent her scurrying back to the car, thinking it was a pity she couldn't look inside while she was there. Unfortunately, it wasn't on the open market yet, so they were hoping Marie's parents would be eager to accept their offer thereby saving estate agent fees.

Giselle switched on the engine grinning ruefully. It was a great opportunity and with an injection of money — and hard graft, it could become a rather nice hotel. She liked the setting very much, and to be fair Blake's appraisal of what would need doing had been spot on as far as she could see. She laughed to herself when she thought of what her father would say. It certainly wasn't going to be any competition for his empire, but she felt in her bones this was something she could do he would understand and appreciate. Time would tell of course, but she couldn't wait to get started on the project. After all it would still be quite an asset so she wouldn't be throwing money away.

★　★　★

Christmas wasn't a bundle of fun. Jason hadn't managed to get leave, which had been a real shame. Giselle had been looking forward to telling him about her proposal and asking his advice. They had always been close and shared hopes, dreams and secrets. He at least understood her ambition to be self-supporting because he felt the same. He promised he would be at her birthday party though, so January 10th couldn't come soon enough. The main problem was Leo Hadleigh who had somehow managed to wangle an invitation to join them for the whole of the ten-day holiday, from just before Christmas until the New Year. Her father said it was because he thought she might like some company of her own age instead of a lot of old buffers, but she knew now there had been a conspiracy between the two families and she was hopping mad. Her father and Seth Hadleigh apparently were old friends, and both thought pairing Giselle with Leo was to be encouraged.

Giselle couldn't believe it. She told her father in no uncertain terms that he was behaving like a Victorian father, marrying his daughter off to his chosen suitor. She made it perfectly plain she wasn't interested in what to her was an arranged marriage, so spent a very uncomfortable few days avoiding everybody. She had so much on her mind and found Leo a severe distraction. He was his usual charming, persuasive self, and tried talking her round. He even refused to accept back the engagement ring, saying he knew he'd been rushing things, and said he'd wait for as long as it took. If it hadn't been for her involvement in the purchase of the Beechcroft, Giselle might have been more co-operative and enjoyed his company — or at least found some Christmas spirit, but she was eager to know if they had succeeded in buying the hotel and was keen to make plans. Blake was going to sound out casually what Marie's folk wanted for the hotel and since he still had a key he was going to let a surveyor in to look around. She hoped he wouldn't come up with too many faults.

She was afraid if she stopped to think about the possibility of failure she would back down. Was it a huge gamble she would live to regret? This was a major turning point in her life — a risky one, but one had to take risks occasionally. Her father had taken risks all his life; he said it kept him on his toes. She missed Blake — his reassuring presence and wished he had come to stay for the holiday, but knew it wasn't his sort of gathering. Although she had only known him a few days, she felt in tune with him. She kept comparing him with Leo, which was a stupid thing to do, as they were total opposites. In the end, Giselle got an early flight back saying she was disgusted with the way they had all been scheming behind her back, and was more than ever determined to go her own way. Marriage wasn't on the agenda for the foreseeable future. She was looking to a career in hotel management not marriage.

★   ★   ★

The purchase of the hotel was going ahead, but it seemed a horribly slow process and she wished the legal requirements were not so protracted. She desperately hoped Blake's in-laws didn't object because of his involvement and put an obstacle in their way. They had tried to keep his name out of any paperwork as much as possible, hoping they would be so pleased to have the hotel sold so quickly they didn't delve too deeply into the buyers.

Giselle spent a lot of time concocting lists of things she thought they would need to do, and learning all she could about running a hotel. Ruefully, she began to realise how complicated her father's business probably was. Granted he had an army of employees taking care of it, but he was still in overall control, and he used to say — the buck stopped with him. Giselle hoped Blake had a good grasp of managing the Beechcroft, but she knew she couldn't rely solely on his knowledge. She had to become conversant herself and wished she had spent more time listening to her father.

There was no way she could avoid the birthday party her father had planned, much as she wished she could. She wasn't in a celebratory mood. Not yet, but to him it was a very special day, when he showed off his grown up daughter to friends and acquaintances. He was even arranging a firework display so she hoped it didn't rain, or worse still snow. Giselle didn't have many friends, just a few school chums to invite, but she did coerce Blake into attending, hoping he would make a favourable impression on her brother Jason. She felt certain the two of them would hit it off. Blake showed great reluctance to attend, so she'd had to do a lot of coaxing and pleading before he agreed. She could well understand what an ordeal it would be for him, but he caved in when she insisted he would be doing her a great favour.

The shindig was being held at the family home — Warren Towers. Not that it felt very homely as far as Giselle was concerned. Ever since her mother ran off with a waiter and gone to live happily ever after in France, the place had been like a show place. It was a well-maintained show place run by an austere housekeeper and numerous staff, but one couldn't call it a home. Giselle couldn't remember the last time they had been together as a happy family group.

To begin with when her mother departed she had been extremely angry, calling her deceitful and dishonest, but latterly had begun to realise her mother had some justification for her actions. Her father was only interested in business and making money so was never at home. She now understood her mother must have been bored out of her skull. Her father would never condone his wife working. In his eyes, she was the lady of the house, and as such should support her husband by socialising and perhaps doing minor charitable work. '*Whatever would people think*?' he used to say, '*If you went out to work? They'd think I couldn't support you in the style to which you've become accustomed.*' Giselle wondered how her shy, reticent mother had eventually summoned up the courage to escape. Father could be so very high-handed and dictatorial, and one had to be pretty determined to stand up to him if you didn't want to be steam-rollered into submission all the time.

Giselle stood alongside her father receiving the guests, a smile held grimly in place. She had learned from an early age one had to toe the line occasionally, and now wasn't a good time to cause an upset.

'You look marvellous, Gigi, quite the lady,' her father murmured. 'Spit and image of your mother, mind. Fortunately, you've got more spunk than her. Must take after me in that department.'

Giselle smiled, surprised by the use of the pet name. 'I guess so, father.' She was not going to resurrect hostilities tonight if she could avoid it. She wished her mother was there. It was the sort of occasion that needed a united family. She hoped her father wasn't thinking of getting married again though. She wasn't sure if she would ever feel comfortable with someone taking her mother's place. Her mother had sent her a beautiful card and present, both hand-made by the look of them but Giselle admired them all the more because of it. Perhaps when things had settled down she would make a flying visit to see her and restore their relationship which had been sorely restrained of late.

During a lull in the proceedings, her father put his arm round her and gave her a squeeze. 'I'm sorry if you think I overstepped the mark with young Leo. I was just being a concerned father, worried you'd have fortune-hunters queuing up now, and wanted to save you . . . '

'It's all right, Dad. I realise your intentions were for the best, but please let me do things my way. I won't squander the money; you can be assured of that. I know what I'm doing.'

He looked at her quizzically. 'Have you something in mind?'

'I'd rather not say for the moment. You always said not to count your chickens . . . '

Her father nodded and chuckled. 'Pity about Leo, I was looking forward to some grandchildren before I get too old to play with them. Sure you won't change your mind? Or is there anyone else in the running I don't know about?'

She laughed. The thought of her father actually interested in children was farcical. Yet, to her surprise he appeared sincere. Giselle hadn't expected to enjoy the party, so was surprised to find that it was going exceedingly well, and even Blake seemed to be looking almost stress-free. She hoped it wasn't an act he was putting on for her benefit, so spent as much time as she could with him to make sure he didn't feel overwhelmed. She knew it wouldn't normally be his sort of scene, but he seemed to be holding his own. Fortunately, as she had expected, Jason found him agreeable company, especially so since Giselle had told Jason of her plan to buy into the hotel trade, and had obtained his unqualified approval. She saw them deep in conversation so wended her way over to them.

'What are you two chatting about?'

'Cars, what else? Father really splashed

out this time. I didn't get a Porsche when I was twenty-one.'

'I seem to recall Dad asked me at the time what he thought you'd want as a present and I said a tank would be most appropriate.'

'See what I mean, Blake,' Jason said. 'She has a way of getting just what she wants, although I suspect the old man has something up his sleeve. The car is a bargaining counter. By the way, what's this I hear about you being able to do decorating and gardening, Gigi?' Jason said drolly. 'I must have had a memory lapse, as I don't recall any such thing.'

'We painted the playhouse if you remember, and planted a flower garden round it. I even got a sunflower to grow . . . it was bigger than yours.'

'Hardly specialist qualifications,' scoffed Jason.

'I can learn.'

'We'll have plenty to practise on at the Beechcroft,' Blake said ruefully, 'especially if we want to be ready for Easter.'

'I'm looking forward to it,' Giselle replied with grim determination. 'I don't mind getting my hands dirty. You should know, Jason. I spent a lot of time handing you greasy spanners and things when you were fixing your bikes.'

Jason gave her a hug and laughed. 'You wouldn't think she was twenty-one would you, Blake? Don't be taken in by her size will you, mate? She's a pint-sized bossy individual who somehow always seems to get her own way come what may.'

Blake gazed down at her and said softly, 'She looks very grown-up to me. Stunningly so. I'd never have recognised you as the same waif I rescued from the snow storm.'

Jason looked startled. 'You rescued my sister from a snow storm? I didn't know that. How come?'

'Rubbish,' Giselle said taking Blake by the arm and leading him away before any more could be said. 'We met purely by chance. I didn't need rescuing. But I do now,' she added and led him out through the patio doors onto the back veranda, picking up a pashmina on the way. 'Leo's been giving me black looks all evening. He suspects you're more than just a friend and is trying to wheedle it out of me who you are.'

It was a crisp, cold night and she wrapped the scarf round her and leant against the balustrade with a sigh. 'You haven't told anyone about our deal have you?'

'What do you take me for? Of course I haven't. The only person I've talked to about it is your brother, because you told me he already knew. He seems happy with the arrangement fortunately. You know I still have reservations and have difficulty in believing it's going to happen. Until we sign on the dotted line, I shan't . . . It sure was my lucky day when you walked into my life. I won't let you down.'

Giselle sighed again. 'I too wish it was all settled. I hate this waiting.'

Blake placed his hands squarely on

the balustrade and stared unseeingly out at the extensive grounds. Giselle came from a different world. Warren Towers was stupendous, and yet she had chosen to visit his humble cottage when she needed a safe haven. It sure was his lucky day, and he knew he would do all in his power to see she was well looked after. She had given him a boost just when he needed it, and had implicit faith they could make the business work. He hoped she was right. Failure wasn't an option. Not when her father was Bunny Warren with all his string of opulent hotels stretching across the world. He'd had many sleepless nights recently wondering if he was doing the right thing, and was truly scared of letting Giselle down, but somehow he knew they should go ahead. They would make it work, even if he had to work twenty-four hours a day. Giselle's cheerful optimism helped of course. He'd never been in such a financially secure position as she was, but recognised having money made quite a difference.

'Giselle, I want to say something. Perhaps now isn't ideal. I know we shouldn't be talking business when we are celebrating your birthday, but I must get it off my chest. I've been giving our involvement a lot of thought over Christmas, and I've come to the conclusion that the only way it will work is if it becomes a proper joint venture. Will you accept Safe Haven as collateral? I don't want to sell it you realise, but I will if I have to. Heaven knows how long it would take to sell anyway. I'm not reneging on the deal. I still want to work with you — but not for you. I hope you understand.'

She nodded thoughtfully. 'Yes, yes I guess I do. You'd feel awkward being beholden to another woman — even me.'

'Not quite how I would have put it, but yes, that is basically it.'

'Marie and her parents scarred you badly didn't they? Well, if that is what you want then so be it, partner.' She stood on tiptoe and kissed him on the cheek. 'I'm so glad I met you, and you're not a homicidal maniac.'

'We'd best be getting back before they miss you, birthday girl,' he said gruffly.

Giselle chuckled sensing her power over him. Maybe he won't be such a pushover as Jason, but . . .

5

The more time Giselle spent with Blake the more she wondered why Marie had been so stupid as to let him go. She considered him wonderful husband material. He was handsome — at least she thought so. He was a diligent worker with a quirky sense of humour she discovered, and also had his romantic side. It had been decided at the outset they would live and work amongst the upheaval — not that they would spend much time in their bedrooms. It was going to be a race against the clock to get the hotel completed in time. However, on the day they signed the contract Giselle received a dozen red roses. Her room was to be at the top of the building under the eaves, and as she placed the vase of flowers on the window ledge she reflected that back home her wardrobe was bigger than this bedroom. It felt slightly claustrophobic, but something she would no doubt get used to.

She was surprised how soon she became accustomed to the rough, simplistic routine. Never before would she have contemplated living almost daily in jeans, a tee shirt and baggy overalls, or going without make-up, hairdos and manicures. She didn't get too worked up when the water was turned off unexpectedly, or there was no hot water for a bath. She was none too happy when there was no electricity though, and the weather had taken a turn for the worse. She was determined to show no sign of weakness and to pull her weight. She was up early every morning, but hardly ever the first down to breakfast. Blake insisted on a full cooked breakfast, which was taken with the rest of the workmen. It gave them time to discuss progress and decide on the priorities for the day.

'I don't believe it,' muttered Blake

one morning scowling at a letter he'd received.

'What don't you believe now?' Giselle said frowning at the paint tin she'd just opened and not caring for the colour.

'Marie's put a hold on the divorce papers.'

'Why?' Giselle asked looking round for a stick to stir the paint.

Blake stuffed the letter back in the envelope and shoved it in his pocket. 'No reason given,' he snapped. 'I suspect she's feeling a bit lost, or fallen out with the current boyfriend or something. Her parents have gone to Spain so now she's all on her ownsome lonesome, which is something she's definitely not used to. She didn't get the job she applied for either, and I know she was distinctly miffed to learn I'm part owner of the Beechcroft. Well she needn't think she can come here with her sob story. I've got more than enough to cope with right now.'

'Think she's having second thoughts and is interested in your marriage working after all then?' Giselle said wryly.

Blake frowned as if it was a novel idea he'd not thought about. 'I can't think why. Not after all she's said in the past. I was never good enough for her, and her parents were dead against me from the start. She said they thought I was too old for her. I'm only ten years older than her for heaven's sake. Marie needed someone mature, who could take charge, because she's not very good at making up her own mind. Her parents always did it for her.'

Giselle grinned. 'Perhaps they influenced her decision initially, but now they've gone to Spain she's unsure of what she really does want. Perhaps she needs a broad shoulder to cry on. You'd better watch out, Blake, she may be back.'

Blake groaned. 'Women!'

Giselle chuckled. She sat back on her heels and looked at Blake with a thoughtful frown on her face. Cautiously she cleared her throat. 'To get back to our present problems,' she said. 'I've been thinking. Don't shout me down straightaway, but how about I speak to my father and ask for assistance? Would you mind?'

Blake raised his eyebrows.

'Yes, I know. I don't really like doing it, but if we are to get the hotel open for Easter in any sort of going condition we need more workmen and pronto. This is a sort of emergency situation isn't it? I just thought Dad has the clout we need.'

Blake shrugged his shoulders. 'If you are sure and you feel like contacting him then go ahead, I've no objections. We could just give everything a lick and a promise to make it look more appealing, but that wouldn't meet your high standards now would it?' he paused. You'll have to come clean about everything though you realise.'

Giselle nodded. 'Yes, I know. I know. Nevertheless, I think it's the only way. Besides I think it is time I told him. It's too late for him to interfere, and we do need a reputable builder, and a more reliable plumber, and more decorators wouldn't come amiss. Time is getting short, and if Dad recommends them . . . '

* * *

The next few weeks passed rather too quickly. There was so much to do. Giselle was as good as her word, and tried her hand at anything that needed doing, but she wasn't used to working fifteen-hour days, and fell into bed thoroughly exhausted. There were days when problems became overwhelming and tempers became short, and on those rare occasions, she wished she had never started the project. Overall though, everything was going to plan, more-or-less. They still bickered over priorities, but on the whole they came to an amicable solution to most problems. Life got ever more hectic as Easter approached.

With less than two weeks to go

Giselle was overseeing the refurbishment of the kitchen, and at the same time supervising some landscape gardeners at work in the grounds. It was quite usual to be doing two jobs at once, and she wondered what her father would say if he could see her now. He had yet to see the hotel for himself. He had asked, but Giselle wanted it to be ready for guests before he visited. She knew he would interfere and make alternative suggestions if he came any earlier, and she didn't want that. This was hers and Blake's endeavour, not one of the Warren empire hotels. It wasn't for the super rich with their fancy ideas, but a modest, more family oriented establishment. It would cater for walkers, ramblers, as well as motoring tourists enjoying the spectacular Lakeland scenery. Somehow she didn't think her father would understand.

A party had been arranged for the following Saturday when hopefully everything would be more or less completed, and it would be a thank you for all those involved in the refurbishment. They had all worked exceptionally hard, and she thanked her lucky stars Blake had been there supporting her. He always appeared so calm in a crisis, and his previous experience of the trade came in useful.

'Will you be inviting Marie to see the improvements?' Giselle asked walking proudly through the refurbished Beechcroft. There was still some titivating up to be completed, but they were only minor details, and wouldn't spoil the atmosphere for the party.

'I might,' Blake murmured, thrilled and proud by what they had accomplished in so short a time. He never thought for a moment they would manage it. It had been damned hard work, often nail-bitingly so, but by some miracle they had completed on time, and had sufficient bookings to make things look extremely promising. He had been amazed at Giselle's resolve. She never gave up. When problems arose she tackled them head on, but of course having the monetary resources behind her made such a difference. Was he being a touch cynical he wondered? 'Are you inviting Leo?'

'Yes, I have to. He's chauffeuring Dad. I'm a bit bothered about Dad, actually. He's not sounding his usual bombastic self these days. I'm sure he's missing Mum, even though he never says so.'

'He's probably been working too hard. Can't you get him to take a holiday? I'm sure we could find him a room.'

Giselle laughed. It felt good to laugh. How long had it been since she felt so light-hearted she wondered? Far too long. She glanced at Blake, wondering what the situation was between him and Marie. They still hadn't got the decree nisi as far as she knew. She wasn't sure what was holding things up, but guessed it was mainly due to Marie. Giselle did wonder if perhaps Blake couldn't have pushed it through more speedily if he had wanted. Did that mean he was still in love with Marie? If Blake were unattached, would it make any difference? For the past few weeks she hadn't given him much thought, but now — today, tidied up for the first time in ages, she saw him for what he was — a rather handsome man and quite a matrimonial catch.

'Why don't we go out somewhere to celebrate, just the two of us?' Blake asked.

'Why not indeed? I think we deserve it. I feel like wining, dining and dancing,' she chuckled.

'You might not be so keen on the dancing when I have trodden on your feet a time or two. I never was one for dancing.'

'I don't believe it, and anyway I'll take my chance.'

It was fun getting ready. Giselle soaked leisurely in a warm scented bath, washed her hair then drifted round the bedroom trying to make up her mind what to wear. She hadn't much to choose from. Eventually she pulled out the dress she had worn for her birthday party. Yes that would do she muttered. It was rather glamorous, perhaps too much so for the locale, but what the heck. Slipping her feet into high-heeled sandals, she smiled at her reflection. She had chosen the highest heels she owned so she would be nearer Blake's shoulder, not his tie-pin when dancing. She envied tall women with svelte figures and long legs, but knew there was not a lot she could do to change herself and compete with them.

Blake was already downstairs when she made her entrance. He gave a long wolf whistle of appreciation making her blush. She had never seen Blake look so distinguished. He had even taken the trouble to slip out and get a haircut, which had taken years off him. Strange she thought, but I don't even know how old he is. I must remember to ask although it didn't really matter, he was Blake — her partner.

'I've ordered a taxi. I hope you don't

mind? I rather fancy having a spot to drink tonight. What say you?'

'Good idea. Time to let our hair down. Where did you have in mind to go?'

'Windermere.'

Half an hour later, they were ensconced at a cosy restaurant that Blake insisted he'd been told was the best in town. There weren't many empty tables which seemed like a good sign and the menu was surprisingly imaginative.

'I don't think I want to see another sandwich, bowl of soup, or scratch meal again,' Giselle said with an impish smile pondering what to order, 'and tonight I fancy a real gourmet meal. Prawn cocktail to start, followed by a mammoth steak, and then I think I will even look at the sweet trolley.'

Blake grinned. 'What to drink?'

'A Martini would go down a treat for starters.'

The drinks arrived and they toasted their achievement. Giselle took a deep breath of appreciation. 'Do you know, Blake, we've known each other for, what over four months, and yet I know little or almost nothing about you. For instance, have you any family? I don't even know how old you are. Please, will you fill me in and tell me a little about yourself?'

Blake shrugged his shoulders. 'Ok partner, but there is not a lot to tell. Let me see. I was born 33 years ago in the cottage where we first met. I was an only child, born to parents rather late in their lives. They are now unfortunately both dead, so apart from some very distant relatives whom I rarely, or should say never see, I am alone in the world. At school, I wasn't what one would call an academic. I was more into doing practical things with my hands. At one time, I did consider becoming a joiner — at school, I enjoyed carpentry lessons, and then I even thought about joining the forces like your brother Jason.

'After I left school I decided to travel

about for a while doing odd jobs here and there, seeing a bit of the world. I travelled right across America, and did a stint in Australia. I even went to India. That was how I became interested in hotel work. It was mainly bar work I did in those days — the easiest jobs to come by, but they were not exactly well paid. It was quite an eye-opener seeing how the rest of the world lives, but eventually I returned to the UK and came to the Lake District. That was five years ago and simply fell in love with it.'

'This really is a beautiful part of the country I must admit,' said Giselle. 'Jason and I used to come here on his motorbike occasionally. We liked to do a bit of fell walking and Jason's done some climbing.'

The waiter arrived with their starters, but Blake continued with his resume. 'I approached the Beechcroft looking for work one fresh spring morning. Fortunately, they needed a general handyman at the time, which of course was right up my street. Marie's parents were in charge in those days, and they employed me.' He tried his soup, but found it too hot so continued. 'It wasn't long before Marie and I started going out together. At first, I thought she really needed to escape her parents' claustrophobic indulgence. However, one thing led to another and a year later we got married. Shortly after that her parents left us in charge, while they, supposedly looked after an elderly relative down south.'

'That must have been quite a responsibility. Marie would only be about twenty.'

'Yes. We got married when she was nineteen — I was twenty-nine. At first, we revelled in the adventure of it all. Marie particularly liked being away from her parents' control. She had been protected, almost smothered all her life. For the first year or so everything was fine, the hotel was doing well and we were enjoying life. Then her parents returned and started to interfere. They didn't approve of the way we, or rather I was operating. They thought there should be more profit to show for our endeavours, even though we were in the middle of a recession. They grumbled about the money spent on refurbishment, but then complained if the hotel was not looking at its best — we just couldn't win. It got to such a pitch it inevitably caused problems between Marie and me because she always tended to side with her parents. When a wife doesn't support her husband in such circumstances then the marriage has no future.'

He poured some wine.

'Do you have any hope..? I mean will you and Marie?'

He shook his head. 'I'm afraid it's irretrievable. I feel sorry for her of course, but I wouldn't want to go through such an upset again, and I don't believe Marie has or will ever grow up. She never has opinions of her own, and relies on everyone else to make decisions for her, so that way she can never be seen to be in the wrong.'

'I'm sorry. That must have been difficult to live with.'

'How about you and whatshis name?'

'Leo? We are still friends. I'm not wanting to be rushed into anything, although my father is still putting pressure on.'

'I rather liked your father.'

'He likes you too. Wanted to know if there was anything going on between the two of us. Still match-making I guess.'

'I presume you put him straight,' he remarked archly. 'I would hate to have him think I was a fortune hunter.'

She laughed. 'Father is more concerned about having grandchildren, mine or Jason's than he is about the money side of things. He's got a bee in his bonnet that he's getting old and thinks grandchildren will somehow make him more youthful.'

Blake frowned. 'If that is all it is.'

'What do you mean?'

'I just thought . . . no, I'd rather not say.'

'Go on spit it out. What about my father?'

'Well, I thought he looked rather — how shall I put it, not exactly in the best of health when I saw him at your party. But it was probably nothing. Jason was a little concerned too I think, but hey I hardly know the man so I probably saw things that aren't there. Forget I said anything.'

Giselle nodded thoughtfully. Her father had lost weight, but she'd thought he'd been spending too much time at some health club trying to recapture his youth. Now she wasn't too sure. She felt guilty because Blake had seen something she had missed.

In the event, they didn't do any dancing, but had a pleasant evening all the same. It was nearly midnight when they returned to the Beechcroft. They stood side by side admiring the refurbished property of which they were undeniably proud.

'Still glad to be half owner?' Giselle asked.

He grinned. 'As long as my collateral isn't in jeopardy I'm happy.'

'Well all the bills haven't yet been paid, but I think we'll just about manage. We've got paying guests booked in for next week don't forget. Actual money coming in for a change. The bank manager will be pleased.'

Blake smiled down at her gamine face made ghostly by the moonlight. Pulling her into his arm, he dropped a kiss on her forehead. 'Thank you, Gigi for having such faith and wisdom beyond your years. You picked me up when I was down in the dumps, and gave me back not only my self respect, but I now have a goal in life. I hope I can return the favour sometime.'

He dropped another kiss on her forehead, but she quickly lifted her head and met his lips with her own. She was more than a little shaken by her own response. She had meant it only as a token between friends, but he was so gentle and truly exciting she felt stunned by her reaction. Blake calmly led her in through the front door without a word, and she half wondered if he was expecting . . .

'Goodnight, Gigi,' he whispered hoarsely and disappeared into the office, leaving her to climb the stairs to her attic bedroom alone.

6

The next morning the talk was all about the opening party celebrations. It was all hands to the helm to get it ready for the fifty or so guests they had invited, including her father, Leo and Marie. Giselle took time out to go shopping for a new dress and to get her hair done. Now she was nervously wondering what her father would make of the Beechcroft. She knew it wasn't in her father's league, but it was a start, and she intended it to be a mere stepping-stone into a whole string of them right across the country. Well a girl can dream can't she? They were aiming at a different market to her father and hoped he would understand and not disparage their hard work.

When she first thought about reno-vating the hotel she had such grand ideas for a very upmarket clientele, similar to her father's. When she had put forward her proposals to Blake however he soon poured cold water on much of what she suggested. Quietly and calmly he had slimmed down her extravagant ideas and pointed out their limited time and resources. He had been right of course, but it still rankled and she resolved to find a more suitable venue for their next project. She wouldn't give up so easily next time. Beechcroft was to be first of many and she felt justifiably proud of what they had achieved.

*   *   *

It was time to go and prepare to meet their guests. With some trepidation she walked down to the reception desk. Blake was already there.

'Gigi, you look adorable,' he remarked with a low whistle of approval.

'Likewise,' she responded admiring Blake's freshly cleaned suit and the new silk shirt she'd given him for his birthday. He looked totally different from the man she had got to know over the past few weeks. They had such a wonderful, almost brotherly relationship that worked well — on the whole. Just occasionally she wished . . . she wasn't quite sure what. She just knew that, in its self, being an hotelier wasn't going to be sufficient, and she wasn't even sure if she was cut out for a career in the business. Now they had completed the hard work and got it up and running she felt almost sad, which was bizarre and didn't make sense. Perhaps it was the thought of Leo and the inevitable decision she had to make that was making her confused.

Marie was the first to arrive looking tall and extremely slim wearing a green sheath dress. It suited her colouring, but Giselle thought she would have looked better with a nice tan. She watched enviously as Blake welcomed her with a kiss on the cheek and led her off for a guided tour. It was only natural she would want to see what changes they'd made to the place that had been her home, but Giselle felt jealous. Why should it matter to me if Marie wants to keep their marriage alive she told herself? For the past few weeks she had got on famously with Blake and was used to him being a free agent, overlooking the fact he was still a married man. As far as she was concerned it was only a matter of time . . . but there was still the possibility they could patch things up. Surely not, she said to herself. Blake had said as much, hadn't he?

Her father and Leo's arrival gave her the diversion she needed away from such dismal thoughts. Tonight was time for partying, although her dad was looking frail she thought. She must remember to ask Jason if he knew if anything was wrong. He hadn't mentioned it last time they had spoken on the phone.

'Hello, Dad. I hope you are going to be suitably impressed, taking into account my lack of experience and the limited time we had available. It's a pity you didn't see it before we started the renovations though, then you would be better able to appreciate the changes we've made,' she added, leading them into the bar area where refreshments were being served.

'It's interesting, has potential,' was her father's guarded wording. 'Good to see you are following in my footsteps, Gigi. Though you are doing it the hard way.'

'I know, Dad, I've heard it all before. I know I could join the company, but I wanted to try to do something on my own.'

Her father's raised eyebrows made her qualify her remark. 'With Blake's help of course. He's been a rock. Turns his hand to anything.'

'Useful guy to have around then. Now do you want any suggestions for further improvements or am I just to say how wonderful everything is and leave it at that?'

Giselle laughed. 'Just be yourself, Dad.'

Overall, the party went well and they received many compliments. As her father left, he said he was delighted with what they had achieved, and reminded her he was always there if she needed any help, financial or otherwise. She smiled her thanks, but knew she would have to be in dire straits for that to happen.

⋆ ⋆ ⋆

The summons she had been half expecting came ten days later. Her father's housekeeper rang sounding extremely agitated. Miss Tindall had been employed at Warren Towers for as long as she could remember and wasn't the easiest person to get along with, but she obviously had her father's well-being at heart.

'He told me not to bother you, but I thought you would want to know. I don't like going behind his back, but he's not at all well, Miss Warren. He's not eating properly, and he's not spent much time in his office like he usually does. He's been prowling round here like a bear with a sore head. To my surprise he actually had the doctor call, to give him the once over he said. I know he's been overdoing things lately, but that's your father for you. Never lets up. I hope I did right in ringing you, but I thought you ought to know how things are.'

'Of course you did the right thing, Miss Tindall. Don't worry,' Giselle reassured her, 'I'll be over as soon as I can. I rather thought something wasn't quite right with him. Like you say he's probably been overdoing things.'

She immediately went to find Blake to tell him he'd obviously been correct and her father was not in good shape after all. She hoped it wasn't too serious, but was exceedingly worried, as she couldn't recall her father ever being ill.

'Go, Giselle. Your father needs you,

and I can manage perfectly well here,' Blake said straight away.

'But . . . '

'I promise to ring and let you know if the roof falls in, or the river overflows and floods us. Otherwise I think we'll survive,' he added sternly.

Giselle smiled her gratitude. 'Thank goodness this didn't happen while we were in the midst of the renovations. I'll probably only be away a couple of days . . . '

'Take whatever time you need. We're not going to be rushed off our feet for the next few weeks, and I'm not exactly helpless you know. You though, need a break, my girl. You've been under quite a strain yourself recently. So why not spend sometime with your father while he's convalescing and kill two birds with one stone?'

Blake was right, although what she really needed was time alone to figure out what her true feelings were for Leo, and Blake. Working alongside Blake for the past few weeks she had grown to appreciate his steady determination and honesty. Now she couldn't envisage a life without him, but on the other hand, she was still sort of in love with Leo. How was it possible to be attracted to two men? Did it mean she wasn't in love with either of them? This was the time she missed her mother. She would have welcomed someone to chat to, even if she didn't take their advice. It wasn't the sort of thing she could discuss with her father that's for sure.

Giselle threw a holdall into the Porsche and drove to Warren Towers in a far from happy state of mind. First of all, she was worried about her father. He'd always been so healthy despite not taking much exercise. She didn't recall him ever having to see a doctor before in his entire life. He installed all the latest equipment in the hotels he owned, but would never dream of using the gym, swimming pool, Jacuzzi or sauna. He'd always prided himself on what a good constitution he had without the need for restraint of any kind. He enjoyed, in moderation, a glass of whiskey and the odd cigar now and then. Nothing excessive. She hoped whatever it was could be soon remedied. She knew he wouldn't be a very co-operative patient. The Porsche ate up the miles and in what seemed like no time at all she was turning into the gates of Warren Towers.

She was relieved to find her father up and about, although looking distinctly pale. He didn't look at all surprised to see her either, so she wondered if he had overheard the conversation with his housekeeper.

'How are you, Dad? From what Miss Tindall said it sounded as if you were heading for a heart attack or worse.'

He shook his head. 'Nothing so dramatic, Gigi. Miss Tindall shouldn't have called you. The doctor says I've got to take it easy for a while that's all. There's nothing for you to worry about, but if it means I have your company then I'll be as ill as you like,' he added with a wry grin.

Giselle laughed, she knew her father hated being pampered. 'Don't bother play-acting on my behalf, but since I'm here I'll stop for a few days. I've some serious thinking to do.'

'You — thinking,' he said with a smile then added. 'Anything I can help you with?'

She shook her head. 'It's sort of personal. We've been so busy recently I haven't had time to think — to decide what I want to do about all sorts of things. You know what it's like. You need to be alone with your thoughts occasionally, but lately there's never seemed a moment for any privacy.'

He nodded. 'I have something personal I wish to discuss with you, Giselle. I don't want to be a nuisance, but I'd welcome your input. Perhaps we can chat over dinner this evening? I've a few phone calls to make, so I'll see you later.'

Giselle wandered out into the grounds wondering what her father wanted to chat about. She hoped it wasn't another attempt to get her to become involved with his business, because she still didn't think she was ready for that, and indeed if she ever would be. It made her look ungrateful she knew, but she agreed with Jason they would prefer to make their own fortune and live the life they wanted without interference. Giselle knew her father would be an exacting and trying person to work for. He always wanted things done his way, and wouldn't listen to anyone else's opinions.

She had a kindly word with the gardener-handyman who was washing her car, and headed off down the drive. She had no clear plan and was so deep in thought she arrived in the village before she knew it. Several people greeted her, which surprised her, as she never got involved with local affairs. Her mother had though. Her mother. She wondered how she was. Was she happy now? How did one know when it was true love and not infatuation?

She arrived at the church and

wandered round the churchyard idly considering her own future. It was a charming village church, highly suitable for a quiet, simple wedding, which was what she would want. Nothing grandiose, just a few invited friends and relatives. The only snag was who was to be the bridegroom? This was putting the cart before the horse. She was young and had no need to rush into matrimony. She could have a career and enjoy her freedom. Everyone kept telling her the world was her oyster . . . she could do exactly whatever she wanted, but somehow it didn't give her any joy. She wanted someone to enjoy it with her. Who was that someone? Was it someone she had already met or a complete stranger like her mother had gone off with. She felt terribly unsettled, and annoyed with herself, so she set off at a brisk pace back to the house to ring Blake.

She slipped easily back into the old routine, and after an invigorating shower, changed for dinner, even though it was only her and her father. She knew he appreciated the effort, and would frown disapproval if she arrived in jeans and a T-shirt. She wished Jason and her mother were present. She did so miss the family atmosphere, teasing Jason about his love life and sparring with her father. Her mother didn't often say much, but she had been very supportive when asked.

She joined her father for a sherry before dinner, keeping the conversation light and inconsequential. During the meal, her father asked how things were at Beechcroft and quizzed her about her next project. She laughed and stressed how capable and efficient Blake was. She remarked how lucky she had been finding such a talented partner, but wouldn't rush into anything else immediately.

They retired to the library for coffee before she talked to him about his problems. 'Now, Dad. What was it you wanted to discuss with me?' she asked eventually. 'I hope it's not another attempt to get me to join the firm, because I think the answer would still be the same. This project of getting Beechcroft up and running has given me food for thought, and made me question what I would like to do in the future. I'm still not sure.'

For once, her father looked a shade uncomfortable. 'No, Gigi. I have accepted your wish to be independent. Both you and Jason have made that perfectly plain, and I respect you for it in a way, although I shall be more than happy if you ever change your mind. After all, eventually it will be for you and Jason to decide what to do with everything when I retire.'

'That's a long way off, Dad. You wouldn't know what to do with yourself if you ever did retire. You know that.'

Her father nodded thoughtfully and cleared his throat. 'Maybe . . . anyway it's like this. I know this might seem I'm asking a lot, but I . . . I sort of wondered if you would do me a huge favour?'

Giselle's eyes widened in surprise. 'Of course I will if I can.'

Looking decidedly uncomfortable, he said somewhat reluctantly. 'You know, regardless of what she's done, I still love your mother. As far as I am concerned there will never be anyone else to take her place, and I'd just like to know if she is happy. I don't know if she keeps in touch with you or Jason. I just want to know she's all right. I do miss her you know.'

'Oh dear, Dad. I'm so sorry for the things I said. At the time I ranted on about a lot of things I now regret. When Mum left I was so confused and dejected, but I realise it must have been a dreadful time for you too. Since she left, I have spoken on the phone to her a few times, and we do exchange the odd letter now and then, but we are hardly close, if you know what I mean? I think she feels embarrassed and rather guilty.'

'Yes, I guess I understand. How would you feel about going to see her, and finding out for yourself if she is truly happy with this fellow Guy? I would hate to think she was miserable and wished to return, but didn't know how. If she is truly happy then I will just have to accept it, but I have a feeling . . . You know I would welcome her back, indeed I'd prefer her to come back where she belongs, here at Warren Towers. It doesn't feel like home without her. She's always been the love of my life. I believe I have learned a few lessons these past few years, and hopefully we could still enjoy a future together. Will you do that for me, Gigi? Tell her I don't care what has happened, what she's done. I just want her home. I'll go and live anywhere she chooses if only she'll come back to me.'

Giselle gulped, not sure how to reply to such an outpouring. It was so unlike her father to admit to being insecure, and she would like to be able to do what he wanted, but it would mean being away from Beechcroft longer than she expected. She wasn't sure how good she would be at negotiating either, although she could see how sincere her father was.

'Of course I'll go. I'll ring Blake and see if I can be spared,' she said with a smile. 'I hate to think I am indispensable, but I suspect he will manage very well whether I am there or not.'

* * *

Two days later Giselle flew to Nice wondering what sort of reception she would receive. On the phone her mother had sounded pleased she was going, although Giselle only said she felt she needed a break now the hotel was up and running. She hadn't mentioned her father at all, preferring to see for herself how things were. She was rather anxious about meeting Guy. If he made her mother happy she should accept it and try to be pleased for them both, but she still felt sympathy for her father. He didn't deserve to be so sad. As far as she knew he had never looked at another woman in all the time they had been married. He could be quite outspoken on the subject of morals and bad manners, which at times had rather grated.

Her mother met her at the airport with a warm hug of delight. 'I was so thrilled to get your call, love,' she said in the back of the taxi weaving through the traffic. 'I'm dying to hear all the news from home. I must admit to being surprised to hear about your latest exploit. I can't imagine what your dad thought.'

'It all happened quite by chance,' Giselle said with a shrug of the shoulders. 'Actually, I really enjoyed the experience. Dad seemed pleased too. He actually said he was proud of me, although it doesn't mean I want to go and work for him. I prefer to do my own thing.'

Her mother squeezed her hand. 'I can understand that. You two would be always clashing heads, you're too alike. How is your father? Is he all right? This is all so unexpected, I hope there's nothing wrong?'

'Father's OK, and no there's nothing really wrong,' Giselle replied cautiously, 'but I'd like your advice, and I thought it was about time we mended some fences.'

Her mother nodded. 'I quite agree. Oh, I am so pleased you've come. We have a lot to catch up with.' The taxi pulled up in front of a block of flats. 'Here we are, home sweet home,' her mother said leaning over to pay the driver.

Giselle looked up thoughtfully. It didn't look a very prepossessing place. The paintwork needed attention, and the flowerbeds desperate for some weeding. It was a far cry from Warren Towers. Her mother led the way up to the first floor with Giselle following on frowning warily. It certainly wasn't the sort of place she had envisaged them living. The building itself was old and not in its first freshness, but her mother's flat turned out to be relatively pleasant inside. Her mother always had the knack of making a homely atmosphere she recalled.

'I hope you'll be comfortable in here,' her mother said showing her into a small single bedroom, simply furnished with a window looking out onto the rear of the building. 'I'll remove the sewing machine if it's in your way.'

'No, don't bother. It's fine, honestly.' Giselle said dropping her case on the bed. 'I'm afraid I can't stay long. Just a few days. I don't want my partner to think I'm leaving him to do all the work so soon.'

Her mother tweaked the curtains and then headed for the door. 'I'll go put the kettle on. Or would you care for some wine?'

'Wine I think,' Giselle said unlocking her case and taking out her nightdress. 'When do I meet Guy?'

Her mother shook her head, looking embarrassed. 'We had a disagreement and he left. Don't worry. I'm fine, really I am. I'll tell you all about it later.'

Giselle was conscious of a growing unease. She quickly tidied herself up and went in search of her mother. She found her sitting on a small balcony overlooking the small shrub-lined square below. There was just room for two chairs and a small table. Her mother had already opened the wine and began to pour a glass for her.

'I like to sit out here whenever I can,' her mother said. 'It helps me unwind.'

'It's lovely,' Giselle replied taking a seat and admiring the view. Now that she had had time to take it in, she could see, although the flat was not very large it was nicely placed, and not too far from the town centre. She guessed the sea front was some distance away though. 'It's lovely to see the sunshine. When I left home it was pouring down and quite cold.'

Giselle didn't know how to broach the delicate subject that was the real reason for her visit, but realised it was probably very pertinent timing.

'You first, Gigi,' her mother said

taking the initiative. 'How have you been these last three years? I heard you didn't want to join 'the firm' and wished to strike out on your own. I can't say I'm surprised. You always were a headstrong lass, determined to do things your way. Jason told me about your partner in this hotel venture. It all sounds very adventurous. Do tell me all about it.'

Giselle laughed. 'It was a pure coincidence actually. I'd better explain. You know I was working for Seth Hadleigh, and so you may also have heard Seth Hadleigh's son Leo asked me to marry him.'

Her mother nodded. 'Yes, I did. I guess I was somewhat surprised. I wouldn't have thought he was your type. You are still rather young. Do you love him?'

'Well, I wouldn't have accepted his ring if I didn't I suppose, but then I discovered they have been plotting behind my back, so I don't know what to believe any more. Dad and Seth connived to bring us together, and I learned from an acquaintance that Leo is particularly interested in my inheritance, and of course the prestige of being a member of the Warren Empire. The only person I seem to have any faith in is Blake, who I know is definitely not after my money.'

Her mother smiled. 'I can see your dilemma. How did you meet Blake? He sounds an interesting character.'

Giselle chuckled. 'I ended up at his cottage in a snow storm and we got talking. He's recovering from a distressing marriage situation, and I had my problems so somehow things clicked. I know he's somewhat older than me, but I feel comfortable with him. He tried his best to put me off ploughing my inheritance into the Beechcroft. He's so solid and reliable. Dad and Jason both seem to like him. That can't be bad now can it?'

Her mother laughed. 'Let me tell you a little about what I know about Leo Hadleigh. His mother and I were sort of school friends. Well, we were both in the same class at school and we moved in the same circles socially. I still hear from her from time to time. From what I understand Leo is actually quite an astute businessman. Don't be deceived by this artistic phase as his mother puts it. He's been rebelling because his father laid down the law and insisted he went to college, or learned a trade, or he would disown him. Leo sensibly took a business course, and passed with flying colours, which pleased Seth no end, but then Leo decided to go walkabout, saying there was more to life than money. He's always been interested in painting. He's very good at it I believe, but this time it was his way of getting back at his father to show him he wanted to choose the way he leads his life, and not have it foisted upon him. Does that all sound familiar?'

Giselle nodded and groaned. 'I wish Leo had told me all this. I've been trying to make up my mind . . . trying to choose between Leo and Blake. I find Blake an honest hardworking, thoroughly charming man, but there has been nothing between us other than a working partnership — well apart from one brotherly kiss. When I first met Leo, I felt . . . felt like we had a sort of empathy. It was only afterwards, when I heard Seth and Dad had somehow instigated our friendship I began to have doubts. The trouble is they are both so different. Leo seems so frivolous and irresponsible in a way, which can be a bit wearing, whereas Blake is more serious, but has a wicked sense of humour when you get to know him. I just wish he wasn't married, although he is supposed to be getting a divorce.'

'It sounds to me as if you both need to take your time to discover if it's true love or merely infatuation, darling. You've all your life ahead of you, so there's no rush.'

'Yes, Mum, I know and thanks, it's good advice.'

'What's holding up Blake's divorce?'

'His wife has had a few personal problems so she's sitting on the paperwork. I really think she's regretting everything and wants Blake back again.'

'I see . . . Do you think they will get back together again?'

'I'm not sure. To begin with, I didn't think there was any doubt about the way Blake felt, but lately I'm not convinced. When we first met he was pretty cut up about the way his in-laws had treated him, but now her parents are in Spain and Marie is on her own he feels sorry for her I think. Anyway, let's forget about that for the moment. Now for the real reason I came.'

He mother frowned. 'So it wasn't just to see me and have the pleasure of my company?'

Giselle giggled. 'Actually, Dad asked me to come. He wants to know if you are truly happy, but what he really, really does want, is for you to return home. He told me there will never be anyone else to take your place, and he

113

misses you like crazy. I ought to tell you also he's had a bit of a scare health-wise. The doctor told him to take things easy, and I believe it came as a bit of a shock. You know, discovering he's not immortal. He now wants to put his affairs in order and spend more time — as the saying goes with his family. He's kept on at me about wanting grandchildren before he gets too old to play with them, would you believe? I don't know if he's psychic or something, but he would dearly love to have you come home. He didn't know Guy had left did he?'

Her mother sat with downcast eyes. 'He may have heard from one of his cronies I suppose.' She shrugged her shoulders. 'I made a big mistake when I left your father. I realised almost as soon as we came here. It was too late by then though. Guy suggested we came to France, where he said he could get better jobs, and funnily enough, it seemed like a foreign country, even though I lived here when I was a child.

I've really missed England, but didn't feel I could return home, not after the way I had treated your father.

'Soon after we arrived I was horrified to discover Guy was a hopeless gambler. Instead of finding a job he spent most of his time in the casinos, and expected me to fund his habit. I know I should have left straight away, but I didn't. I was scared I suppose. I wasn't used to being on my own. I stayed and tried to change Guy, but of course, there was never any chance of that. Once a gambler always a gambler I believe. To begin with he was lucky and had small wins, but then he became hooked in a big way. I ended up pawning my jewellery to keep us afloat, but that didn't last long, and when I had nothing of value left to pawn he left too. I felt so ashamed. For the last couple of years I have been working as a shop assistant — the only job I was capable of doing. In a way I have enjoyed being self-sufficient, but I did feel sad at the

terrible thing I did to you all —
especially your father.

'I don't know what possessed me to
leave you like that. I put it down to the
time of life when feelings go a little
haywire. At the time, I felt like one of
your father's possessions, to be there
when needed, but not valued. I was
tired of the merry-go-round of social
gatherings with all their meaningless
chatter and absurdity. It all came to a
head when I met Guy at a restaurant. I
was supposed to meet your father there,
but as quite often happened he
telephoned to say he'd been held up
and he would see me back at the house
later. Normally I wouldn't have stayed
for a meal, as I disliked dining alone. I
was waiting in the reception area still
undecided and so was Guy. He
remarked we both appeared to have
been stood up so why didn't we share a
table.

'I found him refreshingly charming
and interesting to talk to. It was a very
pleasant meal, but at the end of it, we

went our separate ways and I never expected to see him again. Fate however played a part. By coincidence, I was shopping in Bond Street a week later when who should I bump into but Guy. I thought at the time it was pure accident, but I later learned he had been following me. He could charm the proverbial birds from the trees, and I stupidly fell hook, line and sinker. Anyway, as for returning home, there is nothing I would like better, but I can't. My behaviour has not been honourable, and I wouldn't care to have your father's reputation sullied. I've done him enough damage already.'

Giselle blinked in amazement at the sorry tale. 'You know, Dad wouldn't mind one bit. In fact, he is so miserable if I ring him I think he would be on the next plane out, only I don't think in the present circumstances that would be sensible. I'm not really sure I have heard the truth about how serious his health problem is, so I would hate to cause further anxiety, but honestly,

Mother, he really and truly wants you home.'

Her mother shook her head. 'What can I do? I feel terrible, but I can hardly return with you as if nothing has happened. I do love your father. I always have and always will, but I betrayed his trust.'

'Look, Mum, all I can say is he really wants to see you again. Why not do that at least and see what happens? He's had a lot of time to think, and he's not getting any younger. I wouldn't be surprised if he isn't thinking of early retirement even.'

She could see her mother wavering. 'All right. I'll agree to meet him, as long as it's it somewhere neutral. If it works then fine, but if it doesn't then . . . '

'Then you can take up residence at our hotel in the Lake District. I'll even find you a job if need be.' Giselle went and gave her mother a hug.

'You're very persuasive,' her mother said with a sigh. 'There's a hundred and one things I would have to do first. I shall have to give in my notice at work for a start.'

'I'm sure there is nothing that can't be resolved fairly readily is there?'

Her mother sat looking thoughtful. 'The rent on the flat is paid up until the end of the month. I have it on a short lease.'

Giselle looked delighted. 'Dad will be so pleased. You've no idea how he was almost pleading with me.'

'That doesn't sound like your father. Oh my goodness, I've just realised I haven't been to the hairdresser for months, and clothes are something I sell not buy.' She gave a short laugh. 'I remember when I spent more on one pair of shoes than I spend in a week now on housekeeping.'

'You look great,' Giselle said cautiously, 'but how about tomorrow we hit the shops together? It's been ages since I did any serious retail therapy. I've been too busy getting the hotel refurbished and up and running. I always preferred you to be there with your faultless choice. I never knew what to buy, or what suited me. Oh I have missed you, Mum, and so have Dad and Jason. I do hope it all works out.'

The next day Giselle's mother worked in the morning and then later in the afternoon they went shopping, despite her mother's reticence about using Giselle's credit card. Giselle spent the morning telephoning. First, she rang Blake to find out how he was managing and to say she would be away for a little longer than anticipated. She gave him a condensed version of what had happened, and he responded in his usual relaxed manner that she should take as long as she felt she needed. Next, she rang her father, and since she didn't want to raise his hopes, she gave a guarded reply to his eager questions.

7

They were having breakfast when Giselle broached the subject of her parents' meeting place. 'I can understand you not wanting to return to Warren Towers straight away, and you would prefer neutral territory, Mum. Where had you in mind?'

Her mother frowned. 'I'm not sure. London I guess, and then if it doesn't work out I can stay with some friends in Surrey. That is if I am still welcome there. I seem to have lost touch with so many recently.'

Giselle shook her head. 'That's negative thinking. Let's be more positive shall we? How about the Savoy? Isn't that where the film stars arrange to have their affairs?'

Her mother laughed. 'Why not? It will be nice being pampered again. I used to really enjoy spending a day in

121

town, shopping and visiting the beauty salon.'

Giselle grinned. 'That's more like it. By the way, I didn't know you used a sewing machine. What do you make?'

'Oh, it was a spur of the moment thing. I used to like making soft toys for the village fetes and so on, and I just wondered if there was a market for them. I thought it might be a way I could earn some pin money, that's all.'

'I think that's a marvellous idea. Have you sold any?'

Her mother shook her head. 'I didn't know how to go about finding a market for them. They are just heaped in the cupboard. I'll give them away before I leave.'

'Can I have a look at them?'

'Of course, but I warn you they are not very good.'

'Let me the judge of that,' chuckled Giselle. 'I remember old Nancy, the rag doll you made me when I was about five. I've still got it. I will never part with it for all the tea in China. You could have the beginnings of a cottage industry. Funnily enough I know the very cottage,' she said with a giggle. 'You could even sell them on eBay.'

★ ★ ★

Giselle flew home, keen to set plans in motion. She hoped the planned reconciliation of her parents went ahead without a hitch. She couldn't see a problem there really. They both wanted it to work, so why shouldn't it? Also, she wanted to get orders for her mother's toys, which would give her something to occupy her spare time once she did return home. Knowing her father, no matter what he said he would do, he would find it extremely difficult, if not impossible to relax his business interests. Telling her mother he may be thinking of retiring was a bit of pie in the sky, not really a serious idea. She rather thought her mother realised it too.

As she stepped off the plane, she was

feeling decidedly tired. She wasn't looking forward to the hassle of finding a taxi and the long trip to the Beechcroft or Warren Towers. She couldn't decide where she should go first. She needed sleep.

'Giselle, over here.'

She was delighted to see Leo waving to her from behind the barrier. She collected her luggage and joined him. He gave her a big hug and a kiss.

'Your mother rang and said you could probably do with a shoulder to lean on. She said she had tired you out.'

'I could certainly do with someone to help me sort out my life,' she said simply. 'It seems to be getting more chaotic by the minute.'

'Perhaps I can help. I'm a good listener, you know.'

As they left the airport Giselle was surprised when he headed west instead of east. 'Where are you taking me?' she asked casually, although not too concerned. As long as there was a bed for the night, she didn't care.

'I'm kidnapping you,' he grinned. 'I thought it time we had a serious talk, and also time you became acquainted with my new abode.'

'Gosh, have you bought a place of your own?'

'Yep. I have my very own studio with flat attached. You will be my very first guest. I've been dying to show you it.'

'Who said I was staying?' she asked. 'I have all sorts of things I have to do, and you know I have been away from the hotel for longer than I should. I can't just leave everything to Blake. I know Beechcroft is open at last and we have paying customers, but that isn't the end of my involvement.'

He glared at her. 'They all mean more to you than me then do they?'

'No, of course not. It's just I've . . . I've got commitments. I thought you understood. I told you I need time to sort myself out. I don't want to be rushed into something that will turn out to be a mistake. Can't you understand? I am only twenty one you know, not exactly on the shelf yet.'

He shrugged his shoulders and stamped his foot on the accelerator. The car shot forward and Giselle huddled in her seat trying not to be scared. She'd forgotten how temperamental he could be.

'I'm sorry,' she said when he slowed having caught up another car that refused to move over. 'That was rather thoughtless of me. You must be very excited at having bought a place of your own. I am looking forward to seeing it, providing we get there in one piece that is.'

He slowed the car and turned off the motorway to head for the seaside town of Morecambe. He drove through the town, and along the promenade, before pulling into a parking spot right on the sea front of the bay itself. 'Here we are,' he said with a flourish. 'Leo's Gallery. Do you like it?'

Giselle gazed at the new-ish looking two-storey building and grinned. 'It looks marvellous.' She wasn't too sure about the colour scheme, which she thought a little brash, but didn't want to spoil his enjoyment.

'Wait until you see inside. It's not large, but it's home.' Leo had recovered his good humour and was keen to show her his studio. Tugging her hand he led her into his bijou flat.

Giselle was impressed. 'How did you find such an ideal place?'

He shrugged his shoulders. 'I came here with a friend on a day out and sort of stumbled across it. I just thought what an ideal place it would be for a gallery and set the ball rolling there and then. I've got a huge mortgage on it though, so I'll have to sell a few paintings if I'm to make ends meet. Dad thinks I'm off my rocker of course, but my mum, bless her, thought it worth a shot, and helped me out financially. Don't tell Dad, though.'

'Well, I hope it's a great success, Leo. It looks as if we are both taking risks, in defiance of our fathers doesn't it? We'll just have to prove we can do it.'

He eagerly showed her all the paintings he'd done in preparation for the opening. He had been very busy indeed.

'Now you sit yourself down,' he said eventually, placing her in a comfy old rocking chair with a glass of wine. 'Admire the view while I prepare us a snack.'

Giselle settled herself down with a long sigh and relaxed. It was perfect. The view from the window was stunning. The tide was coming in, and from her vantage point she could see across the estuary to the charming town of Grange over Sands, and further over, the fells of Lakeland glowing in the last rays of the sun. She pondered what Blake was doing, and once again mused about her involvement at Beechcroft. Now the hotel was finished what was to be her role? She couldn't see herself as a waitress or chamber-maid, perhaps receptionist at a pinch, but all in all she preferred all the planning that went before. Perhaps she was more like her dad than she realised. She liked coming up with ideas and planning new ventures, and then it was for others to implement them.

First things first she thought, and made a determined effort to concentrate on Leo. It had been very thoughtful of him to meet her, even if he just wanted to show her his gallery. She yawned thinking about what her mother had told her. She must have dozed off, only waking when she heard Leo calling her name. She stretched and struggled to her feet, surprised to see it was already turning gloomy. She wandered through into the kitchen to see Leo had organised a candlelight supper.

'What did you put in that wine?' she asked smothering another great yawn.

He laughed. 'Come and taste my spaghetti bolognese and see if you approve. It's my own special recipe.'

The evening was delightful with Leo at his most charming. He entertained her with more stories of his exploits on his round the world hitchhiking trip. It sounded as if he had had a whale of a time, albeit short of funds for most of the trip. Giselle wondered if she would have enjoyed such a venture instead of the expensive visits she'd made, staying with friends and had everything arranged for her. She rather doubted she would have survived the arduous bus rides and grotty places he'd had to sleep while apparently working all hours for a pittance. He deserved a medal.

'Where am I going to sleep?' she asked eventually, thinking it was getting too late to leave and find a hotel. She had drunk more wine than usual and was definitely not sober. 'Didn't you say you only have one bedroom?'

He grinned. 'I told you I wanted a serious talk didn't I?'

'I see,' she said wondering what was the best way to handle the situation. 'What was it you wanted to talk about?'

He pulled her onto the sofa and she snuggled up against him sleepily.

'Giselle, I love you, and I'm truly jealous of that hotel manager you've taken up with. I think it's time we . . . you told me where we stand. I have been very patient, and I am prepared to wait as long as need be, but . . . if in the end you mean to marry me. Stay with me tonight, to . . . to show your commitment.'

She looked up at him. He sounded so serious and determined. Most unlike him. Had she misread him? Was he more unsure of himself than she gave him credit for? All she could think to say was she hadn't unpacked her toothbrush.

'Oh Gigi,' he cried. 'I promise I'll make you a good husband. It may take some time before I can give you the lifestyle to which you have become accustomed, but I promise we'll make it. With you by my side the world will be our oyster.'

They were kissing and hugging when the strident ringing of the telephone interrupted them.

'I'd better answer it I suppose,' he said reluctantly breaking away. 'Don't go away. Who ever it is will get short shrift. Goodness, it's getting on for midnight. Who on earth can it be ringing at this hour?'

A short while later he came back and sat heavily down beside her with a great sigh. 'I'm afraid that was bad news. My mother's been involved in a car accident. I'm not sure how serious her condition is, but my father was phoning from the hospital and he's sounding pretty cut up. I'll have to go.'

Instantly Giselle sobered up. 'Oh dear, Leo. What happened? I'll come with you. Which hospital is she in?'

★   ★   ★

Giselle woke with a thick head. She cautiously opened an eye and wondered where on earth she was. Then it all came back to her. She was at Leo's, and in his bed. What had come over her? She lay back recalling how she had agreed to stay the night, and then Leo received the phone call that sent him scurrying south to his mother's bedside. She had volunteered to accompany him, but he said he preferred to go alone, which she could understand. He would have a lot to do family-wise, and she would be in the way, although she could have taken care of the younger children. Giselle sat up and shook her bedraggled hair. She had better get moving. She had things to do too.

First, she rang her father and asked if he would send a car for her. It seemed the best way of escaping Morecambe and her embarrassment. Next, she made herself a strong cup of coffee and wandered round the studio acknowledging Leo's genius. He had done some lovely landscapes as well as portraits. He was talented; there was no doubt about it. He should do well. Would they live over the shop when they were married? She supposed there could be worse places. There would have to be some changes made though. Still time would tell if Leo was the right one for her. With so much going on around her she didn't want to make any hasty decision.

She was about to leave when she spotted his sketchpad lying on the sideboard. Idly flicking through it at random, she was astonished to see quite a few sketches of herself for which she had never posed. Leo obviously could either work from photos or he had a good memory recall. Then she made another startling discovery that certainly set her back. There were three sketches of Marie. She was in no doubt who the subject was even though they had only met once. Why Marie, she wondered? When had they met? Of course it would be at Beechcroft that time. Was he attracted to her she wondered? She wouldn't have thought of Marie as being a typical subject for a painter. She always understood she was a shy sort of person. Although Leo could be persuasive when he really wanted something.

On the way back to Warren Towers, she pondered on the likelihood of Leo being interested in Marie as a partner and not just as a model. The only time they had met as far as she knew was at the opening night party for Beechcroft . . . unless they had met secretly since. The more she thought about it the more relieved she was she hadn't spent the night with Leo. She needed a clearer head before committing herself. Her mother was right; she needed to take her time. She eventually rang Leo to ask after his mother and he said she was likely to be hospitalised for several days. She sent her best wishes and they agreed they would get together again soon. Leo seemed upset she hadn't remained in Morecambe, but she reminded him she had a business to run.

Arriving back home, she gave her father a kiss. 'How are you, Dad?'

'Delighted to have you back, Gigi. So, what news have you? What did your mother say? Is she happy? Is she coming back home?'

Giselle laughed as the walked into the lounge. 'One question at a time, Dad. Mum is fine, although I suspect you already knew on the grapevine Guy had left her?'

He nodded and gave a wry smile. 'Something of the sort.'

'Anyway,' Giselle continued sitting down on the settee. 'For the past two years she has lived alone. She has her own apartment and has been working in a shop in Nice. I told her what you said, that you really wanted her to come home, but she said she didn't want to ruin your reputation. She feels terribly guilty . . . '

'Did you tell her I don't care a jot about the past? We are none of us blameless. I just want her home.'

'Yes, Dad, I told her. Moreover, I think I convinced her, but she said she had things to do first. Don't get your blood pressure up. I really do think she'll be back before long. I do think

. . . perhaps it would be best if it were somewhere neutral. Like a sort of date if you like.'

'Of course, of course.' her father said urgently. 'She only has to say the word and I'll go to Timbuktu if it meant we could be together again.'

Giselle smiled. 'I don't think you'll have to travel quite so far. London maybe.'

★   ★   ★

It was great to see her father looking so much better that Giselle decided it was time she got back to the Beechcroft to see how things were there. She didn't want Blake to think she was skiving. It was marvellous to climb into the Porsche and head for the Lake District. Was it just the feeling of escape, or was it because she would be seeing Blake again she wondered? She had to admit she had missed him. Had his divorce gone through yet? On the other hand, had Marie put a hold on it because she wanted to remain married? Her head was buzzing with questions for which there were no answers. The only thing she did know was she felt safe and comfortable in Blake's company and was looking forward to seeing him again.

She focused on her feelings for Blake, and the more she thought about him the more she knew he was the man she wanted to marry. When she compared him to Leo, she knew there was no contest. Blake was solid and dependable whereas Leo would always be weak and shallow. She didn't look forward to telling Leo of her decision, but knew she would have to do so before too long. The rest of the journey was occupied with thinking up ways to attract Blake to make him notice her for more than just a business partner. Her father would give his blessing, especially with the thought of grandchildren. She was smiling happily to herself when she drew up outside the Beechcroft.

8

Giselle found the chores around the hotel were more complicated than she imagined. She didn't really mind doing a bit of chamber-maiding if it was really necessary, but she drew the line at becoming a waitress. She knew she wouldn't be able to cope with obtaining the orders, and balancing the plates and dishes. She did say she would have a go behind the bar if she was given some tuition, but really when it came down to it now the hotel was up and running she felt all she wanted to do was the office work. Blake in her absence had employed a full time receptionist, and a woman called Alice who came in part time to deal with the paperwork. Alice was super efficient and didn't welcome Giselle's offer of assistance, so she began to feel redundant.

'If it's all right with you I think I'll

pay Leo's mother a visit,' Giselle said a couple of days later. 'I gather she's still in hospital so I suspect it was more serious than Leo implied.'

'Good idea,' Blake said realising she was at a loose end. 'You could call and see your dad as well, to make sure he's organised for his tryst with your mother.'

Giselle laughed. 'I rather like the word tryst. It somehow sounds lovely and old fashioned. They've agreed to meet at the Savoy. I hope the weather stays fine. London has such wonderful parks, and I always think it's nice to get out for a walk if you have things to discuss, don't you?'

Blake looked out of the window at the fells. 'I couldn't agree more. Perhaps one day we might take time out and have a day on the hills.'

Giselle liked the sound of that and told him so.

She left early the next day. It was a long drive down south, but she felt it appropriate to show Leo some support.

Somehow, she still couldn't think of him as her fiancé, even though she thought a lot about him. He came in the same category as her brother, and she was even more grateful for them not having slept together. She may have spent a night in his bed, but not with him in it. She wasn't sure how he would take it when she handed him back his ring, but she knew it was the right thing to do. She imagined he would try to convince her otherwise, but she knew in her heart of hearts she didn't want to marry him now or at any time in the future. Like her mother said she should take her time before rushing into something so momentous as marriage.

Mrs Hadleigh seemed delighted to see her, and received the huge bouquet of flowers with a smile. The private room was becoming like a florist shop. 'I should have thought of something more appropriate,' Giselle said with a grin.

Giselle spent half an hour chatting. She asked after the children, and promised to keep in touch. She told her about her visit to see her mother and about the possibility of her parents getting back together. Mrs Hadleigh said she was thrilled and hoped to see them herself when she was better. As she was leaving the hospital, Giselle met Leo on his way in. He seemed surprised to see her and was somewhat guarded in his greeting.

'I've just been to see your mother. She seems well considering . . . ' she said.

'Yes. She'll be going home soon. Must go, I haven't long . . . parking's a problem and all that.'

'Are you all right, Leo?' She thought he looked shifty.

'Sure. Just got a lot on my mind. You know how it is? Business.'

'Anything I can help you with?' she asked brightly, obviously this wasn't the time to disillusion him about their on off engagement.

'No. Not this time, thanks all the same. Look, I'd better go. I'm running late. I'll give you a ring this evening.'

'Ok. Do that. I shall stop overnight with Dad. Why not ring me there?'

Giselle strolled off to her car wondering what his problem could be. Was it family or work? As she wended her way through the car park, she spotted Leo's car and the passenger seat was occupied. At first she didn't recognise the woman as she had her head down reading a magazine. As she got closer though she was stunned to realise it was Marie — Blake's wife. Giselle was all set to go over and greet her, but then realised why Leo had looked evasive. He was obviously having an affair with Marie. It stuck out a mile. Well, she thought it certainly helped clear the air. Leo was definitely two timing her, so obviously he just had designs on her inheritance. It couldn't be because he actually loved her. She was beginning to think he didn't know what love was. She sat for a moment in her car breathing deeply. She was having difficulty in believing Leo could be so devious. He always sounded so sincere about their relationship. As if he couldn't wait for them to be married. Was he really just interested in her money after all? Surely the Hadleigh's were comfortably off, but of course his father held tight onto the purse strings she'd heard.

Once she had calmed down, she set off for the motorway, deliberating on how best to deal with the recently acquired knowledge, surprising herself at how unperturbed she felt. She was just glad she now knew for certain. Should she confront Leo soon she wondered? Should she in fact tell Blake about Marie's involvement? Did she mind about Marie? No of course she didn't. It meant Blake would soon be free . . . to marry her. She would rather Blake found out for himself though. She wouldn't want to be accused of stirring things up between them.

Two hours later she drew up outside Warren Towers feeling rather weary.

'Hi Dad, how are you?' She kissed

her father and thought he looked appreciably improved.

'Nervous,' he admitted with a grin. 'Your mother's arriving at the end of the week. We spoke on the phone and she sounded fine.'

'It will be all right, Dad. Don't worry. Actually, I bet Mum is as nervous as you are. Anyway, how are you getting on with cutting back on your workload? Have you managed to do anything about it yet?'

'Not really. I promise I'll give it my whole-hearted attention after I've seen your mother. At the moment all I can think about is meeting her again. I mean to make changes though, really I do, but it all depends on her.'

'You mean you could go on a world cruise then?' she chuckled.

'Hmm. I'm not sure if I want to go that far. How's Mrs Hadleigh?'

'Oh, she seems ok. I'm not sure about Leo though.'

'Oh, why so?'

'Well he's been acting mysteriously.

And I do believe he's seeing someone else.'

Her father frowned. 'Got any proof?'

She shook her head. 'You know just before Christmas when I left him, it was because I thought he was wanting to marry me for my money. Everybody said I was imagining it, but I'm beginning to think my first impression was accurate. Why do you think Blake's wife should be sitting in Leo's car outside the hospital waiting for him?'

'You saw . . . Oh, I see. Tricky. I suppose you will just have to ask him. But it does look suspicious I agree.'

'I mean to ask him. That might be him now. He said he would ring this evening.'

Giselle wasted no time in tackling him.

'She . . . she's helping me with the gallery. She was at a loose end so I talked her into assisting me. Didn't I tell you?' he blustered.

Giselle didn't believe a word he said. 'No you didn't,' she snapped. 'The gallery happens to be 100 miles away, so think of another excuse.'

There was a pause. 'She also needed some advice. You know a shoulder to cry on. The divorce and everything was getting her down. Honestly, Giselle. There was nothing to it.'

'Tell that to the marines,' Giselle said slamming down the receiver.

Giselle left the next day eager to get back to Beechcroft. 'I'll be keeping my fingers crossed for you, Dad,' She said as she kissed her father goodbye. 'You will ring me won't you? And don't forget Mum likes yellow roses not red ones.'

Giselle arrived back at Beechcroft still undecided as to whether she should mention to Blake having seen Marie with Leo, but decided not to. There was no doubt in her mind that Marie was probably chasing after Leo, and he seemed agreeable to the arrangement. Whatever, she'd had enough. The first thing she did when she got to her room was to parcel up the engagement ring.

This time he could have it back for good. Then she went in search of Blake. She found him in the office staring at the computer screen.

'What's been happening here in my absence, partner? You looked worried.'

'Oh, nothing too serious, Giselle. It's nice to have you back though. We are a little short handed because I had to give one of the waiters his marching orders. He was rude to a customer and didn't get on with the rest of the staff. I think he would have turned out to be a troublemaker. Also one of the waitresses left without letting me know — she just walked off, otherwise everything is tickety boo.'

'Nothing too serious then?' Giselle said with a smile.

Blake chewed his lip. 'Well, there is something else I should mention. I know this isn't an ideal request, but I need to take some time off.'

Giselle was taken aback, but managed to hide her unease. 'No problem. I'll cover for you. It's time I pulled my weight. I've had quite a bit of time off recently, you must be due some r&r.'

Blake nodded thoughtfully. 'Thanks, but it will be no picnic. I don't really want to go, but I don't see I have any alternative. The thing is Marie's in a bit of a stew. She rang me very early this morning. Her parents, you recall, went to live in Spain. Apparently, they bought a block of holiday flats with a small café on the ground floor. To cut a long story short, they were attacked and ended up in hospital.'

'Good heavens. Are they going to be all right?'

'I expect so. I suppose Marie has been exaggerating as usual, but she's in a panic and wants me to fly out there with her. I don't know what she expects me to do apart from hold her hand, but I'll be back as soon as I can, I promise.'

'Of course you must do what you can to help,' Giselle said with a slight shrug of the shoulders. 'I should be able to hold the fort here until you get back. I'm not totally incapable you know.'

Secretly she was appalled and hoped it wouldn't mean Marie got her claws into him again, and he deciding their marriage was worth saving. Sun, sangria and sex went together didn't they?

'Sorry,' he grinned. 'I know Beechcroft is in very capable hands with you, partner.'

'When are you thinking of going?'

'I'd like to make tonight's late night flight from Manchester if possible. By the way I think Paul can cope alone if you do need to leave at all. I made him assistant manager with an increase in pay. I hope you don't mind.'

Giselle readily agreed. She was beginning to realise she didn't want to be involved in the day-to-day running of the hotel. She had other things on her mind. 'You go and pack and I'll run you to the airport. I presume you are to meet Marie there.'

'If you're sure . . . '

'Of course. Now go. I'm quite sure Paul and I will manage perfectly well without you bossing us around.'

The next few days Giselle was on tenterhooks, hoping Marie and her parents wouldn't talk him into some wild scheme of theirs to stay on in Spain. She knew she was being illogical, but she wouldn't rest until he was safely back at the Beechcroft. Even though he rang her regularly, and sounded as if he was missing her, she couldn't settle. She was delighted to learn Marie's parents hadn't been kept in hospital. They were back at their flat recuperating, so they couldn't have been too badly injured.

Blake reported they had asked him to take over the running of the café, but he had steadfastly refused. He suggested Marie was perfectly capable of such a responsibility, and he even found them someone local to assist her, but said he had his own business to see to. Once he was sure his presence was no longer required, he phoned to say he would be on the next flight home. Giselle was thrilled and arranged to pick him up at the airport.

9

Giselle felt restless and anxious, wondering how her parents were getting on and where she stood with Blake. Since his return from Spain he'd been quiet and thoughtful. He'd not said anything about the divorce, and much as she would like to have asked him about it, she didn't think she could. He did say the property in Spain was quite appealing, and he thought it a sensible buy, and of course the weather was a wonderful inducement, all of which she could understand, but she hoped it didn't mean he wanted to go and live there. She didn't think he would want to renege on their agreement, which would mean him having to sell his cottage, but still . . . People did change their minds didn't they? What would she do if he did want to end their arrangement? She didn't want to be left looking after the hotel on her own. To be quite honest she didn't want to spend much time dealing with the day to day running of the place. She had enjoyed the excitement of acquiring it and the refurbishing, but now it all seemed rather dull.

During the next few days, Blake spoke to Marie often on the telephone and seemed to be getting along too cosily from Giselle's point of view. She was also fretting about her parents, wondering if they would get back together. She really hoped they would. She loved them both and hated to see either of them hurt.

'They'll be fine,' Blake kept telling her, but with little effect. Eventually he growled at her. 'Why don't you go for a walk? It will take your mind of things, and will do you good. You said you'd done some fell walking in the past, so perhaps it's time you saw what is on your own doorstep.'

Giselle frowned thoughtfully. She realised she was being a pain. 'What about you? I seem to have done nothing but skive since the hotel opened for business, while you have been slaving away. It's you that should be having time off.'

Blake sighed. 'Ok then, if we can get Paul to do the morning shift tomorrow why don't we both escape? Will that suit you?'

'That would be great . . . if you are sure?'

'Of course. It's time we gave Paul more responsibility. I think he will make a good manager one day and doesn't want us breathing down his neck all the time. Besides Tuesday mornings are not usually too onerous.'

The following morning turned out to be one of those glorious sunny days with hardly a breath of wind. The fells looked incredibly beautiful as Giselle drew back the curtains. She was determined to enjoy her day alone with Blake and see if she could make any progress with finding out how he felt about Marie. If he seemed at all unwilling to finalise the divorce, then she would have no option but to accept he was still in love with Marie, and she would reluctantly have to retreat. She couldn't remain at Beechcroft. It would be too uncomfortable. What would she do then? She dreaded to think about it. Why did life have to be so complicated?

In the kitchen, Blake was already preparing the sandwiches and a flask of coffee, which he stowed in a rucksack.

'Morning, Giselle. Ready to conquer the mountain?' he asked with a grin.

'No sweat,' she responded, 'once I've had breakfast of course. I need my nourishment.'

Soon after nine they left the hotel. Blake set a leisurely pace as they meandered through the trees before starting the path up the hillside. Giselle was eager to show Blake she was more than capable of keeping up with his long strides, but he strolled along not in any hurry. As the path grew ever steeper she was relieved by the leisurely pace.

'I must say we couldn't have chosen a

better day,' he remarked stopping once again to admire the view.

Giselle was by now beginning to wish she'd spent more time exercising and was glad of the respite. She definitely wasn't as fit as she thought she was. Fortunately there were numerous views they had to admire so they could make many stops.

'Is it much further?' she asked eventually, breathing deeply and feeling her legs were tiring of the uphill struggle.

'The top? No, not far now. Glad you came?' he chuckled, putting an arm round her shoulders to urge her on. 'You are not doing too bad for a city girl.'

'It's not fair. I have to take twice as many steps to you. No wonder I'm puffed,' she retorted.

He laughed, but did slow down a bit. 'You're doing fine . . . for an amateur.'

She pulled a face and dug him in the ribs. 'You're not doing to bad for an old man.'

'An old man am I? Well, I guess to a young twenty-one year old I am.'

'Did you ever come up here with Marie?' she asked.

'Good heavens no. This isn't Marie's idea of a day out. She'll tramp for hours round the shops in silly high heels then complain her feet hurt, the thought of even a stroll round the village was asking too much.'

Giselle smiled inwardly and felt her step lightening. They scrambled up the next steep slope only to find the summit was still not in sight.

'I thought you said we were nearly there,' she muttered.

'Come on. Not much further. Just over the next rise. I promise you it's worth it.'

Giselle was beginning to wonder, especially when she considered they had to go all the way back down again. There were no taxis around here and very few other walkers either.

Eventually they made it and stood together by the cairn admiring a truly panoramic view. They could see for miles in all directions.

'That's really something,' she said quietly; glad to have made the effort.

After a while Blake took her by the hand and led to a grassy hollow to shelter out of the stiff breeze blowing across the top. 'Time for some lunch I think. You deserve it. You did very well.' He opened the rucksack and took out a rainproof sheet, which he proceeded to spread out for her to sit on. When she was settled he sat down next to her and unpacked the rest of the foodstuff. He handed her a packet of sandwiches and poured coffee out of the Thermos. 'I expect you're ready for that.'

'I certainly am. I'm ravenous.'

They sat in companionable silence for a while as they ate. When they were both replete he lay back and stretched out his long legs with a sigh. 'This is the life. It was a good idea of yours I think.'

'What was? Acquiring a hotel and spending weeks renovating it?' she grumbled. Giselle looked down at him and smiled. 'Hey, lazybones. What do we do now? Got any plans?'

He groaned. 'After a siesta we wander back the same way we came up, or if you prefer we can do a detour. It's a shade longer, but makes a pleasant change.'

'Hmm. I'm in your hands. You decide.' With that she stretched out herself and closed her eyes. They lay like that for a while, but then Giselle got fidgety and propped herself up on her elbow and leaned over him. 'Blake?' she said and stopped.

'Hmm,' he said sleepily.

'I . . . what . . . I mean, what do you truly think of me?'

He opened his eyes and gazed into hers. 'How do you mean?'

Giselle chewed her lip, not sure how to carry on. 'Well, am I just a business partner, or is it possible we could be . . . well you know.'

He sat up and pulled her into his arms. He kissed the top of her head and murmured, 'Would you be interested if

I said I'd like to think we had more going for us than the business?'

She snuggled up to him and sighed softly. 'I think I'm in love with you.'

She felt him heave a sigh too. 'Is that so? How long have you been thinking that?' he said gently stroking her face. Not waiting for a reply, he went on, 'I presume you haven't forgotten about Leo?'

She pushed herself away and stared out at the scenery, feeling tense and embarrassed. 'I have a confession to make. I've been in a quandary ever since we met. I wouldn't call it love at first sight, but you've grown on me until now I don't want ever to be apart from you. When I'm away I spend all my time wishing you were with me. I feel happy and more content when I'm with you. I am jealous of Marie and hoped you wouldn't decide to remain married to her. I guess I really do love you, and want to know if you feel the same about me? As for Leo, I sent the two-timing low life his ring back. He's been stringing me along while all the time he was seeing another woman.'

'Oh Giselle, my darling girl. I'm so sorry. Do you know who it is?'

She grimaced and shrugged her shoulders, loath to say.

He sighed. 'I don't suppose it's Marie by any chance is it?'

She nodded. 'Oh, so you knew. Why didn't you tell me? I've been dying to tell you.'

He looked thoughtful. 'It was none of my business to interfere, or so I thought. I guess I may have said something if you'd started planning a wedding, but from what you have said previously I didn't think that was in the offing. In actual fact I've been waiting for you to say something.'

Giselle grinned ruefully. 'You and Marie are definitely getting a divorce then?'

'Oh yes. The decree absolute should be through any day.'

'So there's nothing to stop us getting to know each other a little better?'

'I rather like the sound of that, darling . . . only I still have this problem of you being so wealthy and me a penniless vagabond.'

'You are nothing of the sort,' she snapped, and punched him. 'You still have Safe Haven, and Beechcroft is going to be extremely profitable, given time. Besides, my father likes you; he says he likes the cut of your gib.'

'What a strange expression.'

'Dad's a Yorkshireman, believes in saying what he thinks, and has some quaint expressions I admit. Oh well, in for a penny, in for a pound. I'm not sure if this is an opportune time to mention it, but Dad asked me to ask you if you would consider a managerial job with Warren Enterprises?'

'Gigi!' he sounded totally stunned. 'Is this your doing?'

'Oh no,' she laughed. 'Dad sensed how I felt about you, and hopes to entice you into the family circle. He's still after those grandchildren, you know.'

'I really don't know what to say.'

'Say you'll marry me and take the job. You'd be very good at it, and would be in Dad's good books for ever more.'

'But we hardly know each other,' he protested jokily. 'I have no qualifications. Can I have the job even if I don't marry his daughter?'

She pulled a face.

'Only joking,' he said squeezing her tightly and kissing her with such tender gentle lips that she sighed happily. 'Maybe I should rephrase that. Do I have to take the job if I marry his daughter? Do you come as a complete package?'

She reached up and kissed him back so it was some time before she answered. 'Blake Conrad I love you and want to marry you. Since it's leap year, and although we are well passed February 29th' I'm asking you to marry me? As for the job proposition, you'll have to argue that out with father. It's for you to decide. He can be a hard task master as I'm sure you are aware. Jason and I both kept well away from joining the firm because we didn't want to feel we got the job for who we were and not on our own merits. If you know what I mean.'

Blake struggled to free himself from her embrace. He stood up as if to collect his thoughts and stared thoughtfully at the view, but as soon as a couple of fell walkers had gone past he bent down on one knee, took Giselle's hand in his and kissed it. 'Giselle, my darling. Will you do the honour of becoming my wife? To have and to hold until death do us part?'

She smiled happily, before throwing herself at him and shouted, 'Yes, my love, yes, yes, yes. I will marry you.'

'Once will do,' he murmured, and they were once again kissing each other regardless of who was watching.

It was some little while before they set off back down the hill chattering all the way about future possibilities.

'I don't know what sort of job you

think I can do for the Warren Empire. I don't actually have any real qualifications you know.'

Giselle grinned. 'I think Dad wants you to follow up something I mentioned to him. You know, of course, Dad's business is targeted at the exclusive jet setting people, but I wanted to find a string of smaller hotels like Beechcroft. When I told Dad of my plans he immediately saw the potential. We'd need to scout around for likely hotels we can renovate like we have just done, but with the Warren Empire's backing. It should be fun don't you think?'

Blake was shaking his head in bewilderment. 'You take my breath away. There was I, a humble hotel manager with no credentials or prospects, and you walked into my life. Within a few short months, you have turned my simple existence upside down. All I can say is if it will make you happy, my darling, I'll willingly work for your father, and I promise to do my very best not to let you down.'

'He's not really such an ogre,' Giselle said ruefully. 'Actually he'll be thrilled to have family involvement at last.'

As they approached the Beechcroft, Giselle spotted her father's car in the car park. She pointed it out to Blake.

'Good timing,' he said with a wry, apprehensive grin. 'No time like the present I suppose.'

'I hope it means good news,' Giselle replied putting a spurt on. She couldn't get her boots off fast enough as she rushed in to the hotel. She was relieved to see both her mother and father sitting in the coffee lounge, and surprised to see they were actually holding hands.

'Hi,' she said giving them both a kiss. 'How are things?'

He mother smiled and squeezed her hand. 'You were right, darling. You make a good matchmaker. We just dropped in to tell you I'm home to stay — thanks to you.' She then looked towards the door, and Giselle turned to see Blake hanging back not knowing whether he should intrude.

'I'll be in the office if you need me . . . '

Before he could escape, she went over and took him by the arm, smiling encouragingly she dragged him in. 'We have a lot to celebrate. Mum, I'd like you to meet Blake. It's time you two met because Blake and I have just got engaged.'

She heard her father chuckle as he got to his feet. 'Welcome to the family, son. Goodness knows what sort of life you'll lead with this feisty daughter of mine, but it won't be peaceful that's for sure.'

Blake shook his hand. 'I think I know what to expect,' he replied with a twinkle in his eye. He turned to Giselle's mother to say how very pleased he was to finally meet her.

As they were leaving a short while later, Giselle's father took Blake to one side. 'I really am delighted to have you aboard, and no doubt Gigi will have mentioned I have an opening in the Company I hope will interest you. Perhaps we can get together before too long to discuss it?'

'It will be a pleasure, sir,' Blake said, 'but at the moment I am still stunned by how quickly Giselle and I have become engaged. We went out this morning with nothing further from my mind than to climb yon fell overlooking the hotel.'

Mr Warren chuckled. 'Giselle has a way of making things happen, doesn't she?'

Meanwhile Giselle was telling her mother about her toys being displayed in the local shop window, and maybe she should get on with making some more before they all sell out.

Later that evening as they walked by the river, Blake asked Giselle where she thought they would live. 'There's always Safe Haven of course. Although it's not really suitable for a family.'

Giselle chewed her lip thoughtfully, before replying. 'There's an apartment over the stables at Warren Towers we could have. It would need some refurbishment of course . . . '

Blake pretended to look annoyed. 'I see. You have been planning this for quite a while haven't you? What other schemes have you up your sleeve I ought to know about?'

She gave him a hug. 'Not schemes exactly. I rather like the idea of us working together . . . until the children come along. If we lived in the grounds then we'd have ready-made baby sitters, and the children would have a nice, safe place to play. Until recently I thought I would like a career, but I've suddenly become all broody and want to get started on those grandchildren my father's always on about.'

'Do I have a say in this?' he growled.

'Oh I hope so. I do hope so. You won't make me wait too long for a honeymoon will you?'

'You know, Giselle, you're incorrigible. It's supposed to be the bridegroom who is impatient.'

'Well, aren't you?'

'Yes,' he whispered. 'Oh yes, my darling Giselle.'

10

'Telephone call for you, Giselle,' Paul said passing her the handset. 'Some guy who said it's personal.'

Giselle stood back to view the flower arrangement she had just completed. 'Giselle Warren. Can I help you?'

'Giselle, thank heavens.'

'Leo,' she responded coldly, instantly prepared to put the phone down. 'We've got nothing to say to each other. I thought I had made that abundantly plain.'

'Please, Giselle, I am at my wits end. I guess you haven't heard yet, but my father's died of a heart attack. I'm desperate.'

That startled her. 'Good heavens. No. I'm really sorry, Leo. I didn't know. How is your mother coping?'

She heard him sigh. 'Ok. Sort of. Mum's recovered quite well from her accident, but she could do with some help now with my brother and sister. There's so much to see to.'

'Can't you . . . ?'

'I'm up to my eyes looking after the Company. I can't be in two places at once. Please, Giselle, could you possibly help us out for a few days? I wouldn't ask, but I've nowhere else to turn. Now isn't the time to employ a complete stranger.'

Giselle pondered for a minute. She knew Blake wouldn't be too happy if she went, but she did feel great sympathy for Leo's mother in the circumstances. 'I am rather busy myself at the moment,' she said, 'but I'll see what I can do. I'm not promising anything mind. I'm so very sorry for you all, and I'll certainly do what I can.'

'Thanks,' he muttered and the line went dead.

How awful, thought Giselle. Seth Hadleigh wasn't as old as her father. It certainly made one think. She went to find Blake.

'No, Giselle. You can't keep running off like that. I'm as sorry as you are for the Hadleighs, but we have a business to run. Have you forgotten the wedding party due in at the weekend, we'll need all available hands, and we are supposed to go and see your father next Monday remember?'

'Dad will understand,' Giselle said quietly. She knew Blake was right, and she had taken more time off than she should, but she still felt she should go, even for a couple of days. 'I feel a sort of obligation to Mrs Hadleigh.'

'Not Leo I suppose?'

'No,' she snapped. 'I told you I never wanted to see him again. But this is different.'

'How is it different pray?'

'Leo will be at the offices. I'm going to help his mother.'

'I'm sure the exalted Hadleighs will have as much help as they need, Giselle. You are required more here.'

Giselle turned and walked out of the hotel without another word. She was furious. Who was he to remind her of her duties? If it wasn't for her money and ideas he wouldn't be where he was today. He could damn well manage for a couple of days without her help. She was going. Why shouldn't she? By the time she had her temper under control she was near the river, and finally, finding a vacant seat slumped down. Recently Blake had become a bit difficult about a few things, which wasn't like him. He was normally a very calm, equitable guy. She wondered if he was having second thoughts about marrying her.

'There you are,' Blake said sliding into the seat beside her. 'I'm sorry. I shouldn't have snapped at you.'

She looked at him sadly. 'Having second thoughts about becoming involved with the Warrens?'

He shook his head. 'No of course not. Only, I am anxious about making a good impression with your father.'

She sighed. 'Is that all?'

He put his arm round her waist and

drew her close, but she resisted. He sat back with a sigh. 'You father rang shortly after you left. Apparently, Seth's funeral is on Monday so he needs to cancel our appointment anyway. He suggested we all go down to London together. We can be there and back in a day.'

'You happy with that?' she growled.

'Look, Giselle, I know you still have some feelings for Leo, so if you really do want to spend some time with the Hadleighs I won't stand in your way. Perhaps it would be best if you did — resolve things once and for all. I don't want the spectre of Leo Hadleigh to be there for ever after we're married.'

'It won't be, because like I told you it's over between Leo and me. I would be perfectly happy if I never laid eyes on him again. Marie's welcome to him.'

'Ok. I believe you. I expect we are both a bit on edge at the moment what with one thing or another. I think you

175

ought to know, according to your father, Seth's heart attack was probably self-induced as he was facing bankruptcy.'

Giselle gasped. 'I don't believe it. Why? How?'

'The grapevine suggests Seth was being investigated for malpractice. No doubt Leo is now trying to find an easy way out of the tricky situation he has been landed with. You were the first person he thought of as usual.'

'Seth was bankrupt? I can't believe it.' Giselle said thoughtfully.

'That's what you father said. He also said he'll have a word with Leo and see if there is anything he can do, but he's not going to throw good money after bad.'

Giselle sighed. 'This is worse than I thought. Mrs Hadleigh must be devastated. You say the funeral is on Monday? Of course, we'll have to attend that. You will go too won't you? You said you knew Seth.'

'Yes, I told your father we would both be there.'

'I'll see how things are and decide then whether to stay to help. I promise you it will only be for a very short time to see them over the worst and then I am all yours, my darling.'

'OK. I'll hold you to that. One more thing I'd like you to seriously consider. Perhaps while you are away you will have time to decide. I've just received a cheque. A very large cheque, and wonder if it would be best if I buy the Beechcroft complete or are we thinking about selling it in the near future? What with all that's been going on recently I don't know if I am on my head or my heels.'

Giselle stared at him in disbelief. 'What . . . how? I mean where did it come from?'

He laughed. 'Nothing illegal I assure you. I've had my first ever win on the football pools.'

'Wow,' she said with a grin. 'How large?'

'Enough to feel a little more comfortable about marrying you.'

'That much,' she said with a chuckle and hugged him tight.

11

Mrs Hadleigh welcomed Giselle with open arms. She seemed overwhelmed by the whole unhappy situation, and professed to know nothing about what her husband had done. She knew nothing about his business affairs and concentrated purely on running the household. Giselle tried her best to calm her down and involved her with the children who were somewhat naturally bewildered. She didn't feel she could turn her back on her former employer, but dreaded the occasions when she was alone with Leo. He was floundering, obviously, and tried to get back into Giselle's good books, while she was having none of it.

'Where's Marie?' she demanded. 'Surely if she thought anything about you she would be here now, helping you and your poor mother.'

Leo slumped down and held his head in his hands despairingly. 'She said her parents needed her, so she's back in Spain. She took off the minute the press started gathering. I did hope she would at least look after the gallery for a while, but no she was off like a bullet. She's not at all like you, Giselle. I knew I could rely on you, thank goodness.'

'Not for long, Leo. I have my own business to run don't forget.'

'Your partner can do that can't he?'

'Why on earth should he?'

Leo smirked. 'It would look good in the eyes of your father. After all you're a very wealthy woman and he's . . . '

'That's enough. *You* may have proposed marriage to get your hands on my money, but not Blake. He's far too principled to do that, and for your information it was me that proposed to him.'

Leo simply shrugged his shoulders, 'If you say so, but I believe different. Especially having spoken to Marie. She would give you a very different story.

He's not such a saint as you make out.'

'Oh give me strength,' she snapped and flounced out of the room. It was time to head home. Time to spend with Blake planning their future. Why do I keep letting him get to me she thought? Leo's nothing but a waste of space. Blake was not a money-grabbing monster. He's thoughtful and decent. Why, he even put his cottage up as security didn't he? But . . . maybe he thought I wouldn't be interested in it. Maybe he thought he could have a cushy life as Leo suggested. No, I don't believe it. I can't wait to get back and have him hold me in his arms again. I love him and I'm sure he loves me.

* * *

Once she was sure the Hadleighs could manage she packed and left. She promised Mrs Hadleigh she would keep in touch, but didn't really mean it. It was a great relief to set off for home. Unfortunately it seemed to take an age with lots of hold ups on the motorway and roads flooded on the more minor ones. She had been out of touch with any news for several days and it took her by surprise. Apparently there had been very stormy weather up north and she hoped all was well with everyone. She did consider calling to see her parents but felt she would rather go straight to Blake, with no more delay.

Finally she turned into the village and drew up outside the Beechcroft. With a sigh of relief she sat for a moment and then noticed how quiet everything was. There were no cars in the car park, no people wandering about. Where were the guests? What had happened? She spotted Paul about to get in his car, and called out to him.

'Hello, Miss Warren. It's a sad business,' Paul said.

'Why? What's happened? Where is everybody?'

Paul looked embarrassed. 'Sorry. I forgot. You weren't told. Blake said not to worry you in the circumstances.

Things have been a bit chaotic these last few days.'

'Told what, for goodness sake. What's been going on?'

'Well, there was a fire. The hotel was too badly damaged to remain open.'

Giselle was appalled. 'Was anybody hurt?'

'No, only Blake. He has superficial burns.'

'Oh my goodness. Is he all right? Where is he? Why didn't someone ring me?'

'Blake said not to disturb you, said there was nothing you could do. He did all that was necessary — with your father's help I believe, but until we can get some workmen in the hotel has had to close.'

Instinct told Giselle that Blake would head for Safe Haven, which was where she went next. She was appalled at what had happened, and felt guilty for not being there when she was needed. It was very late by the time she turned in to the track leading to Safe Haven and she smiled thinking about the last time she had done so. She coasted to a stop just short of the cottage, noting the absence of any light at the windows. She contemplated the options open to her if the key wasn't still under the plant pot. She was desperate to see Blake and find out how badly he'd been hurt.

The key was in its place thank goodness. Quietly she opened the door and tiptoed up the stairs. Unfortunately the door creaked noisily and woke him.

'What are you doing here?' Blake asked in astonishment as she entered the bedroom.

'Seems to me we've been through all that once before,' she replied with a chuckle.

Blake struggled to sit up making her aware of his bandaged hands.

'Oh my heavens,' she gasped, and launched herself at him. 'You should have rung me. Why didn't you? I should have been there. Are you all right?'

He did his best to gather her into his

arms and kissed the top of her head. 'There was nothing anyone could do, so there was no point in worrying you, my love.'

'What actually did happen?' she asked snuggling up to him.

He leaned back against the head-board and sighed. 'It was all my fault. I take full responsibility for it. I feel terribly guilty. You know that waiter I fired for being a troublemaker; well he returned one night — or rather early one morning and set fire to the dining room. The fire spread to one of the bedrooms, and caused all sorts of mayhem. I understand he'd been working at another hotel and they had also fired him so he was getting his own back.'

'That doesn't mean it was your fault, Blake darling.'

'Maybe not officially, but I still feel I should have been more alert. By the way your father's been a brick. He managed to relocate all our guests, at least all those we couldn't find rooms for in the village. I'm afraid it will be a little while before Beechcroft is back in action.'

'So, now we have plenty of time to organise our wedding then,' she murmured snuggling down under the covers, too tired to get undressed.

Blake sighed, smiling with contentment. Life with Giselle would never be boring, but he looked forward to many happy years together.